MURDER ON THE THIRTY-FIRST FLOOR

Per Wahlöö

Translated from the Swedish by
Sarah Death

CHIVERS

British Library Cataloguing in Publication Data available

This Large Print edition published by AudioGO Ltd, Bath, 2013.
Published by arrangement with the Random House Group Limited

U.K.   Hardcover   ISBN   978 1 4713 1470 4
U.K.   Softcover   ISBN   978 1 4713 1471 1

AudioGO● 1 5 FEB 2013

Printed and bound in Great Britain by
MPG Books Group Limited

For Maj

CHAPTER 1

The alarm was raised at exactly 13.02. The chief of police phoned the order through personally to the Sixteenth police District and ninety seconds later the alarm bell sounded in the operational rooms and administrative offices on the ground floor. It was still ringing when Inspector Jensen got down from his room. Jensen was a middle-aged police officer of normal build, with an unlined and expressionless face. On the bottom step of the spiral staircase he stopped and let his eyes scan the reception area. He adjusted his tie and went out to his car.

The midday traffic was heavy, a mass of gleaming sheet metal, and the buildings of the city, a maze of glass and concrete pillars, rose from the stream of cars. In this world of hard surfaces, the people on the pavements looked homeless and dissatisfied. They were well dressed but strangely identical, and all of them were in a hurry. They swarmed on their way in jerky queues, clotting at red lights and fast-food outlets of shiny chrome. They looked constantly about them and fiddled with their briefcases and handbags.

Sirens wailing, the police cars bored through the crush.

Inspector Jensen was travelling in the first

1

vehicle, a dark blue, standard-issue, PVC-panelled police car; it was followed by a van with grey bodywork, bars at the windows of the rear doors and a flashing light on the roof.

The police chief came through via the radio control room.

'Jensen?'

'Yes?'

'Where are you?'

'In front of the Trades Union Palace . . .'

'Have you got the sirens on?'

'Yes.'

'Turn them off as soon as you're through the square.'

'The traffic's really bad.'

'It can't be helped. You've got to avoid attracting attention.'

'The reporters are tuned in to us all the time, anyway.'

'You needn't worry about them. I'm thinking about the public. The man in the street.'

'Understood.'

'Are you in uniform?'

'No.'

'Good. What manpower have you got with you?'

'One, plus four from the plainclothes patrol. And then the police van, with an additional nine constables. In uniform.'

'Only those in plain clothes are to show themselves inside or in the immediate vicinity

2

of the building. Have the van set down half the men three hundred metres before you get there. Then it can drive straight past and park higher up, at a safe distance.'

'Understood.'

'Close off the main street and the side roads leading into it.'

'Understood.'

'If anyone asks, the closure's for emergency roadworks. Something like . . .'

He tailed off.

'A burst pipe in the district heating system?'

'Spot on.'

There was a crackle on the line.

'Jensen?'

'Yes.'

'You'll remember about the titles business?'

'The titles business?'

'I thought everybody knew. You mustn't refer to any of them as Director.'

'Understood.'

'They're very sensitive on that point.'

'I see.'

'I'm sure I don't need to re-emphasise the delicate nature of the operation?'

'No.'

A mechanical rushing sound. Something that could have been a sigh, deep and metallic.

'Where are you now?'

'The south side of the square. In front of the workers' monument.'

'Turn off the sirens.'

3

'Done.'

'Space the vehicles out more.'

'Done.'

'I'm sending all available radio patrol cars as backup. They'll come up to the parking area. Hold them in reserve.'

'Understood.'

'Where are you?'

'The highway on the north side of the square. I can see the building.'

The road was broad and straight, with six lanes and a narrow, white-painted traffic island along the middle. Behind a tall, wire-mesh fence running along the western side there was an embankment, and at the bottom a vast long-distance lorry depot with hundreds of warehouses and white and red trucks queuing at the loading platforms. A number of people were moving about down there, mainly packers and drivers in white boiler suits and red caps.

The road ran uphill, cutting through a ridge of solid rock that had been blasted away. Its eastern side was a wall of granite, its irregularities smoothed over with concrete. It was pale blue, with rusty vertical stripes caused by the reinforcement bars, and just visible above it were the tops of a few leafless trees. From down below you couldn't see the buildings beyond the trees, but Jensen knew they were there, and what they looked like. One of them was a mental hospital.

At its highest point, the road came level

4

with the top of the ridge and curved slightly to the right. And that was where the Skyscraper stood; it was one of the tallest buildings in the country, its elevated position making it visible from all over the city. You could always see it there above you, and whatever direction you were coming from, it seemed to be the point towards which your approach road was leading.

The Skyscraper had a square layout and thirty floors. Each of its façades had four hundred and fifty windows and a white clock with red hands. Its exterior was of glass, the panels dark blue at ground level, fading gradually to lighter shades on the higher floors.

To Jensen, peering through the windscreen, the Skyscraper seemed to shoot up out of the ground and grow into the cold, cloudless spring sky.

Still with the radio telephone pressed to his ear, he leaned forward. The Skyscraper enlarged to fill his entire field of vision.

'Jensen?'

'Yes.'

'I'm relying on you. It's your job now to make an assessment of the situation.'

There was a brief, crackling pause. Then the police chief gave a hesitant:

'Over and out.'

CHAPTER 2

The rooms on the eighteenth floor were carpeted in pale blue. There were two large model ships in display cases and a reception area with easy chairs and kidney-shaped tables.

In a room with glass walls sat three unoccupied young women. One of them glanced in the visitor's direction and said:

'Can I help you?'

'My name's Jensen. It's urgent.'

'Oh?'

She rose lazily, crossed the floor with light, practised nonchalance and opened a door: 'There's someone called Jensen here.'

Her legs were shapely and her waist slim. Her clothes displayed no taste.

Another woman appeared in the doorway. She looked a little older, though not much, and had blonde hair, distinct features and a generally antiseptic appearance.

She looked past her assistant and said:

'Come in. You're expected.'

The corner room had six windows and the city lay spread below them, as unreal and lifeless as a model on a topographical map. In spite of the dazzling sun, the view and visibility were superb, the daylight clear and cold. The colours in the room were clean and hard and the walls very light, as were the floor covering

6

and the tubular steel furniture.

There was a glass-fronted cabinet between the windows, containing silver coloured cups, engraved with wreaths of oak leaves and borne aloft by bases of black wood. Most of the cups were crowned with naked archers or eagles with outspread wings.

On the desk stood an intercom, a very large stainless steel ashtray and an ivory coloured cobra.

On top of the glass-fronted cabinet was a red-and-white flag on a chrome stand, designed for tabletop use, and under the desk there were a pair of pale yellow sandals and an empty aluminium waste-paper bin.

In the middle of the desk lay a letter, marked special delivery.

There were two men in the room.

One of them was standing at one end of the desk, his fingertips resting on the polished surface. He was wearing a well-pressed dark suit, hand-stitched black shoes, a white shirt and a silver-grey silk tie. His face was smooth and servile, his hair neatly combed and his eyes almost canine behind thick, horn-rimmed glasses. Jensen had often seen faces like that, particularly on television.

The other man, who looked somewhat younger, was wearing yellow-and-white-striped socks, light brown trousers and a loose white shirt, unbuttoned at the neck. He was kneeling on a chair over by one of the windows with his chin in his hand and his elbows resting on the white marble sill. He was blond and blue-eyed and had no shoes on.

Jensen showed his ID and took a step towards the desk.

'Are you in charge here, sir?

The man in the silk tie shook his head deprecatingly and backed away from the desk with slight bowing movements and vague but eager gestures towards the window. His smile defied analysis.

The blond man slid from the chair and came padding across the floor. He gave Jensen a short, hearty shake of the hand. Then he indicated the desk.

'There,' he said.

The envelope was white, and very ordinary. It had three stamps on it and, in the bottom left hand corner, the red special delivery sticker. Inside the envelope was a sheet of paper, folded in four. Both the address and the message itself were composed of individual letters of the alphabet, obviously cut out of a newspaper or magazine. The paper seemed to be of extremely good quality and the size looked rather unusual. Jensen held the sheet between the tips of his fingers and read:

as a reprisal for the murder committed by you a powerful explosive charge has been placed on the premises it has a timer and is set to detonate at exactly fourteen hundred hours on the twenty-third of March let those who are innocent save themselves

'She's mad, of course,' said the blond-haired man. 'Mentally ill, that's all there is to it.'

'Yes, that's the conclusion we've reached,' said the man in the silk tie.

'Either that or it's a very bad joke,' said the blond man.

'And in unusually poor taste.'

'Well yes, that could be the case, of course,' said the man in the silk tie.

The blond-haired man gave him an apathetic look. Then he said, 'This is one of our directors. Head of publishing . . .' He hesitated momentarily and then added,

'My right-hand man.'

The other man's smile widened and he inclined his head. It might have been a greeting, or perhaps he was lowering his head for some other reason. Shame, for example, or deference, or pride.

'We have ninety-eight other directors,' said the blond man.

Inspector Jensen looked at his watch. It showed 13.19.

'I thought I heard you say "she", Director. Do you have reason to suspect the sender is a woman?'

'I'm usually referred to simply as publisher,' said the blond man.

9

He ambled round the desk, sat down and put his right leg over the arm of the chair.

'No,' he said, 'Of course not. I must have just happened to phrase it that way. Someone must have put together that letter.'

'Just so,' said the head of publishing.

'I wonder who?' said the blond man.

'Yes,' said the head of publishing.

His smile had vanished and been replaced by a deep, pensive frown.

The publisher swung his left leg, too, over the arm of his chair.

Jensen looked at his watch again. 13.21.

'The premises must be evacuated,' he said.

'Evacuated? That won't be possible. It would mean stopping the whole production line. Maybe for several hours. Do you have any idea what that would cost?'

He spun the revolving chair round with a kick and fixed his right-hand man with a challenging look. The head of publishing instantly furrowed his brow still further and started a mumbled calculation on his fingers. The man who wanted to be referred to as a publisher regarded him coldly and swung himself back.

'At least three-quarters of a million,' he said. 'Have you got that? Three-quarters of a million. At least. Maybe twice that.'

Jensen read the letter through again. Looked at his watch. 13.23.

The publisher went on:

'We publish one hundred and forty-four magazines. They're all produced in this building. Their joint print run comes to more than twenty-one million copies. A week. There's nothing more important than getting them printed and distributed on time.'

His face changed. The blue eyes seemed to grow clearer.

'In every home in the land, people are waiting for their magazines. It's the same for everyone, from princesses at court to farmers' wives, from the top men and women in society to the down-and-outs, if there are any; it applies to them all.'

He paused briefly. Then went on. 'And the little children. All the little children.'

'The little children?'

'Yes, ninety-eight of our magazines are for children, for the little ones.'

'Comics,' clarified the head of publishing.

The blond man gave him an ungrateful look, and his face changed again. He kicked his chair round irritably and glared at Jensen.

'Well, Inspector?'

'With all due respect for what you've just told me, I still think the premises should be evacuated,' Jensen said.

'Is that all you've got to say? What are your people doing, by the way?'

'Searching.'

'If there's a bomb, then presumably they'll find it?'

11

'They're extremely competent, but they've very little time at their disposal. An explosive charge can be very difficult to locate. It could be hidden practically anywhere. The instant my men find anything they will report directly to me here.'

'They've still got three-quarters of an hour.'

Jensen looked at his watch.

'Thirty-five minutes. But even if the charge is found, disarming it can take some time.'

'And if there isn't a bomb?'

'I must still advise evacuation.'

'Even if the risk is assessed as small?'

'Yes. It may be that the threat won't be carried out, that nothing will happen. But there are unfortunately instances where the opposite has occurred.'

'Where?'

'In the history of crime.'

Jensen clasped his hands behind his back and rocked on the balls of his feet.

'That's my professional assessment, anyway,' he said.

The publisher gave him a long look.

'How much would it cost us for your assessment to turn out to be a different one?' he said.

Jensen regarded him stonily.

The man at the desk appeared to resign himself.

'Only joking, of course,' he said grimly.

He put his feet down, turned the chair to

12

face the right way, rested his arms on the desktop in front of him and crumpled forward, his forehead slumping on to his clenched left hand. He pulled himself upright with a jerk.

'We'll have to confer with my cousin,' he said, pressing a button on the intercom.

Jensen checked the time. 13.27.

The man in the silk tie had moved, silently, and was standing close beside him. He whispered:

'With the boss, the top man, the head of the whole trust, the chairman of the board of the entire group.'

The publisher had been mumbling a few quick words into the intercom. But his attention was back on them now, and he gave them a cold look. He pressed another button, leaned towards the microphone and spoke, in a rapid, businesslike fashion.

'Site manager? Make the calculations for a fire drill. High-speed evacuation. We need the timings within three minutes. Report directly to me.'

The chairman came into the room. He was blond, like his cousin, and about ten years his senior. His face was calm and handsome and earnest, his shoulders broad and his posture very upright. He wore a brown suit, and appeared simple and dignified. When he spoke, his voice was deep and its tone muted.

'The new one, how old is she?' he asked absent-mindedly, with the faintest of nods towards the door.

'Sixteen,' said his cousin.

'Wow.'

The director of publishing had drawn back towards the glass-fronted cabinet and looked as though he were standing on tiptoe, though he wasn't.

'This man's a police officer,' said the publisher. 'His people are carrying out a search but not finding anything. He says we've got to evacuate.'

The chairman went over to the window and stood motionless, looking out.

'Spring's here already,' he said. 'How beautiful it is.'

You could have heard a pin drop in the room. Jensen looked at his watch. 13.29.

'Move our cars,' said the chairman out of the corner of his mouth.

The director of publishing made for the door at a run.

'They're right beside the building,' the chairman said softly. 'How beautiful it is,' he repeated.

Thirty seconds of silence elapsed.

There was a buzz, and a light flashed on the intercom.

'Yes,' said the publisher.

'Eighteen to twenty minutes using all sets of stairs, the paternoster lift system and the automatic high-speed elevators.'

'All floors?'

14

'Not the thirty-first.'

'So the . . . Special Department?'

'Would take considerably longer.'

The voice from the machine lost something of its efficient tone.

'The spiral staircases are narrow,' it said.

'I know.'

Click. Silence. 13.31.

Jensen went over to one of the windows. Way below him he could see the parking area and the wide, six-lane road, now a deserted strip. He could also see that his men had blocked off the carriageway with bright yellow barriers about four hundred metres from the Skyscraper and one of the officers was busy diverting the traffic down a side street. In spite of the distance, he could clearly see the policemen's green uniforms and the traffic constable's white armbands.

Two extremely large black cars were pulling out of the parking area. They were driven away, heading south, and followed by another one, which was white and presumably belonged to the director of publishing.

The man had slipped back into the room and was standing by the wall. His smile was an anxious one and his head was drooping under the weight of his thoughts.

'How many floors does this building have?' said Jensen.

'Thirty above ground,' said the publisher. 'Plus four below. We usually count it as thirty.'

15

'I thought you mentioned a thirty-first?'

'Well if I did, it must have been absent-mindedness.'

'How many staff are there?'

'Here? In the Skyscraper?'

'Yes.'

'Four thousand one hundred in the main building. About two thousand in the annexe.'

'So over six thousand in total?'

'Yes.'

'I must insist they are evacuated.'

Silence. The publisher spun once round on his desk chair.

The chairman stood with his hands in his pockets, looking out. He turned slowly to Jensen. His regular-featured face wore a grave expression.

'Do you really consider it likely that there's a bomb in the building?'

'We have to allow for the possibility, at any rate.'

'You're a police inspector, aren't you?'

'Yes.'

'And have you ever come across a case like this before?'

Jensen thought for a moment.

'This is a very special case. But experience tells us that the claims made in anonymous letters do correspond with reality in eighty per cent of all known cases or are at the very least based on facts.'

'That's been statistically proven?'

16

'Yes.'

'Do you know what an evacuation would cost us?'

'Yes.'

'Our company has been wrestling with financial difficulties for the last thirty years. Our losses are increasing year on year. That is unfortunately also a statistical fact. We have only been able to continue publishing our titles at the cost of great personal sacrifice.'

His voice had taken on a new ring, bitter and complaining.

Jensen did not reply. 13.34.

'Our operations here are entirely non-profit-making. We're not businessmen. We're book publishers.'

'Book publishers?'

'We view our magazines as books. They answer the need that the books of earlier times never succeeded in fulfilling.'

He looked out of the window.

'Beautiful,' he mumbled. 'When I walked through the park today, the first flowers were already in bloom. Snowdrops and winter aconites. Are you an outdoor person?'

'Not particularly.'

'Everyone should be an outdoor person. It would make life richer. Richer still.'

He turned back to Jensen.

'Do you realise what you're asking of us? The cost will be enormous. We're under a lot of pressure. Even in our private lives. Since last

17

year's results were announced, we only use large boxes of matches at home. I mention that as just one little example.'

'Large boxes of matches?'

'Yes. We're having to make savings wherever we can. Larger boxes work out considerably cheaper. It makes good economic sense.'

The publisher was now sitting on the desk with his feet on the armrests of the chair. He looked at his cousin.

'Maybe it would make good economic sense if there really were a bomb. We're growing out of the Skyscraper.'

The chairman regarded him with a mournful expression.

'The insurance will cover us,' said the publisher.

'And who's going to cover the insurance company?'

'The banks.'

'And the banks?'

The publisher said nothing.

The chairman turned his attention back to Jensen.

'I assume you're bound by official secrecy?'

'Of course.'

'The chief of police recommended you. I hope he knew what he was doing.'

Jensen had no answer to that.

'Presumably you haven't got any uniformed officers inside the building?'

18

'No.'

The publisher pulled his legs up on to the desk and sat cross-legged, like a tailor.

Jensen took a surreptitious look at his watch. 13.36.

'If there really is a bomb here,' said the publisher. 'Six thousand people . . . Tell me, Mr Jensen, what would the percentage loss be?'

'The percentage loss?'

'Yes, of staff.'

'That's impossible to predict.'

The publisher muttered something, apparently to himself.

'We might be accused of blowing them sky high on purpose. It's a question of prestige. Have you thought of the loss of prestige?' he asked his cousin.

The chairman's veiled, blue-grey eyes looked out over the city, which was white and clean and cubic. Jet planes drew linear patterns in the spring sky.

'Evacuate,' he said out of the corner of his mouth.

Jensen noted the time. 13.38.

The publisher stretched out a hand to the intercom and put his mouth close to the microphone. His voice was clear and distinct.

'Fire drill. Implement high-speed evacuation. The building is to be empty within eighteen minutes, with the exception of the Special Department. Begin ninety seconds

19

from now.'

The red light went out. The publisher stood up. He clarified:

'It's better for the people on the thirty-first floor to stay safely in their department than to be marching down the stairs. The power supply's cut the moment the last lift reaches the ground floor.'

'Who can wish us such harm?' said the chairman sadly.

He went out.

The publisher started putting on his sandals.

Jensen left the room with the head of publishing.

As the door closed behind them, the corners of the director's mouth fell, his expression grew stony and arrogant and his eyes sharp and searching. As they walked through the office the idle young women crouched over their desks.

It was exactly 13.40 as Inspector Jensen stepped out of the lift and emerged into the lobby. He gestured to his men to follow him and went out through the revolving doors.

The police left the building.

Behind them, voices from loudspeakers were echoing between the concrete walls.

CHAPTER 3

The car was stationed right up against the wall of rock, halfway between the police roadblock and the car park.

Inspector Jensen sat in the front seat, next to the driver. He had a stopwatch in his left hand and the radio microphone in his right. He issued an almost constant series of gruff, terse messages to the policemen in the radio patrol cars and at the roadblocks. His posture was straight-backed, the grey hair at the back of his neck neat and close-cropped.

In the back seat sat the man with the silk tie and the variable smile. His forehead glistened with sweat and he shifted uneasily in his seat. Now, with neither superiors nor inferiors in the vicinity, his face was at rest. Its features were slack and apathetic, and a spongy, pink tongue occasionally flickered over his lips. He had presumably overlooked the fact that Jensen could see him in the rearview mirror.

'There's no need for you to stay here if you find it disagreeable, sir,' said Jensen.

'I've got to. The chairman and the publisher have both left. That leaves me in charge.'

'I see.'

'Is it dangerous?'

'Scarcely.'

'But if the whole building collapses?'

21

'It seems unlikely.'

Jensen looked at the stopwatch: 13.51.

Then he looked back to the Skyscraper. Even from this distance, more than three hundred metres away, it looked awe-inspiring, overwhelming in its magnificent height and solidity. The white sunlight was reflected in four hundred and fifty panes of glass, set in identically uniform metal frames, and the blue facing of the walls looked cold, smooth and uncaring. It crossed his mind that the building really ought to collapse even without explosive charges, under its own enormous weight, or that the walls ought to explode from the sheer pressure compressed within them.

Out through the front entrance pushed an apparently endless column of people. It wound its way in a slow, wide loop between the rows of cars in the parking area, continued through the metal-barred gates in the tall wire-mesh fence, down the slope and diagonally over the grey concrete apron of the lorry depot. At the far side of the loading platforms and long, squat rows of warehouses it broke apart and dispersed into a diffuse grey mass, a fog bank of people. Despite the distance, Jensen could see that about two-thirds of the employees appeared to be women and that most of them were wearing green. Presumably it was this spring's colour.

Two large red trucks equipped with hose reels and turntable ladders drove on to the

22

forecourt and pulled up a short distance from the entrance doors. The firefighters sat in rows along the sides and their steel helmets glinted in the sun. Not a sound had been heard from their sirens or alarm bells.

By 13.57 the stream of people was thinning out, and a minute after that, only a few stray individuals were emerging through the glass doors.

A few moments later, just a single figure, a man, was to be seen at the entrance. Straining his eyes, Jensen recognised him. It was the head of the plainclothes patrol.

Jensen looked at the stopwatch. 13.59.

Behind him he could hear the nervous movements of the director of publishing.

The firefighters remained in their seats. The solitary policeman had vanished. The building was empty.

Jensen took a final glance at the stopwatch. Then he stared at the Skyscraper and started the countdown.

Past fifteen, the seconds seemed to stretch and get longer.

Fourteen . . . thirteen . . . twelve . . . eleven . . . ten . . . nine . . . eight . . . seven . . . six . . . five . . . four . . . three . . . two . . . one . . .

'Zero,' said Inspector Jensen.

23

CHAPTER 4

'This is an unprecedented crime,' said the chief of police over the telephone.

'But there was no bomb. Nothing happened, nothing at all. After an hour the fire drill was called off and the staff went back to work. By four o'clock or earlier, everything was back to normal again.'

'None the less, it is an unprecedented crime,' said the chief of police.

His voice was insistent, with a hint of entreaty, as if he was trying to convince not only the person he was addressing but also himself.

'The perpetrator must be caught,' he said.

'The investigation will naturally continue.'

'This can't be any old routine investigation. You've got to find the culprit.'

'Yes.'

'Now listen here a moment. I don't want to criticise the steps you took, of course.'

'I did the only thing possible. The risk was too great. It could have meant the loss of hundreds of lives, maybe even more. If fire had broken out in the building as a result of an explosion there wasn't much we could have done. The fire brigade's ladders only reach the seventh or eighth floor. The firefighters would have had to attack it from below and the fire would have

24

carried on spreading upwards. What's more, the building's a hundred and twenty metres tall and at heights above thirty metres the jumping nets are useless.'

'Of course, I understand all that. And I'm not criticising you, as I said. But they're very upset. The shutdown allegedly cost them nearly two million. The chairman's been in personal touch with the Minister for the Interior. He didn't exactly lodge a complaint.'

Pause.

'Thank God, no official complaint.'

Jensen said nothing.

'But he was very upset, as I say. By both the financial cost and the chicanery they've been exposed to. That was his precise word: chicanery.'

'Yes.'

'They demand that the perpetrator be apprehended at once.'

'It may take time. The letter's our only lead.'

'I know that. But this matter's got to be cleared up.'

'Yes.'

'It's a very sensitive investigation, and not only that but also, as I say, extremely urgent. I want you to clear your desk of everything else right away. Whatever else you're busy with can be considered non-essential.'

'Understood.'

'Today's Monday. You've got a week, no more. Seven days, Jensen.'

25

'Understood.'

'I'm putting you in personal charge of this. Naturally you'll get all the technical support staff you need, but don't give them any details about the case. If you need to confer with anyone, come straight to me.'

'I dare say the plainclothes patrol already has a fair idea what's been going on.'

'Yes, that's very unfortunate. You must insist on their complete discretion.'

'Of course.'

'You must conduct any essential interviews yourself.'

'Understood.'

'One other thing: they don't want to be disturbed by the investigation while it's in progress. Their time is at a premium. If you consider it absolutely vital to ask them for information, they prefer to communicate it to you through their chief executive, the director of publishing.'

'Understood.'

'Have you met him?'

'Yes.'

'Jensen?'

'Yes?'

'You've got to pull this off. Not least for your own sake.'

Inspector Jensen hung up. He rested his elbows on his green blotter and put his head in his hands. His short grey hair was rough and bristly to the touch of his fingertips. He had been on duty now for fifteen hours, it was 10 p.m. and he was very tired.

He got up from his desk chair, stretched his back and shoulders, and went out into the corridor and down the spiral staircase to the reception area and duty desk. Everything down there was old-fashioned and the walls were painted the same grass-green colour he remembered from his own time as a patrol officer twenty-five years before. A long wooden counter ran the length of the room, and beyond it were some wall-mounted benches and a row of interrogation booths with glass screens and smooth, round doorknobs. At this time of day there were few people in the guardroom. A few escaped alcoholics and starving prostitutes, all middle-aged or older, sat huddled on the benches waiting for their turn in the booths, and behind the desk sat a bare-headed police officer in a green linen uniform. He was the one on telephone duty. Every so often there was the sound of a vehicle rumbling in through the archway.

Jensen opened a steel door in the wall and went down to the basement. The Sixteenth District station was an old one, virtually the only old building still standing in this part of the city, and in a pretty poor state of repair, but the arrest cells were newly built. The ceilings, floors and walls were painted white and the barred doors gleamed, etched in the bright lights.

27

Outside the door to the yard stood a grey police van with the back doors open. Some uniformed constables were emptying it of its passengers, shoving a collection of drunks into the building for a full body search. They were dealing very roughly with their charges, but Jensen knew it was more out of exhaustion than brutality.

He passed through the search area and looked into the drunks' naked, desperate faces.

Despite the strict clampdown, public drunkenness was rising from year to year, and since the government had forced through a new law making alcohol abuse an offence in the home as well, the burden of police work had assumed almost superhuman proportions. Every evening between two and three thousand individuals were arrested, all more or less blind drunk; around half of them were women. Jensen recalled that back in his time as a patrol officer, they had thought three hundred drunks on a Saturday night was a lot.

An ambulance had pulled up alongside the van, and behind it stood a young man in a cap and a white coat. It was the police doctor.

'Five of them need to go to hospital and get their stomachs pumped,' he said. 'I daren't keep them here. I can't be held responsible if anything should happen to them.'

Jensen nodded.

'What a bloody mess it all is,' said the police

doctor. 'They slap five thousand per cent duty on booze. Then they create living conditions that force people to drink themselves to death, and to crown it all they earn three hundred thousand a day in fines for drunkenness, in this city alone.'

'You need to watch your tongue,' said Inspector Jensen.

CHAPTER 5

Inspector Jensen lived relatively centrally, in a housing area south of the city, and it took him less than an hour to drive home in his police car.

In the city centre the streets were quite busy; the snack bars and cinemas were still open and the pavements were full of people strolling past the rows of lighted shop windows. The people's faces looked white and tense, as though pained by the cold, corrosive light of the street lamps and advertising signs. There were occasional groups of young people gathered idly around popcorn stalls or in front of shop windows. Most were just standing there and did not seem to be talking to each other. Some of them cast indifferent glances at the police car.

Youth crime, previously considered a serious problem, had decreased in the last ten years and had now been almost eradicated. There was less crime generally, in all categories; it was really only alcohol abuse that was on the rise. At several places in the shopping area, Jensen saw uniformed officers at work. Their white rubber truncheons glinted in the neon light as they pushed those they had arrested into the police vans.

He drove down into the road tunnel by the Ministry of the Interior and came back up eight kilometres later in an industrial area empty of people, crossed a bridge and continued south down the motorway.

He felt tired and had a dull, nagging pain in his diaphragm, on the right-hand side.

The suburb where he lived comprised thirty-six eight-storey tower blocks, set out in four parallel lines. Between the rows of apartment blocks there were car parks, areas of grass, and play pavilions of transparent plastic for the children.

Jensen pulled up in front of the seventh block in the third row, turned off the ignition and got out into the cold, clear, starry night. Although his watch showed it was only five past eleven, all the blocks were in darkness. He put a coin in the parking meter, turned the knob to set the red hour hand, and went up to his flat.

He switched on the light and took off his outdoor clothes, shoes, tie and jacket. He unbuttoned his shirt and walked through from

30

the hall, letting his eyes rest briefly on the impersonal furnishings, the large television set and the police training college photos hanging on the walls.

Then he let down the blinds at the windows, took off his trousers and switched off the light. He went out into the kitchen and took the bottle from the refrigerator.

Inspector Jensen went to get a tumbler, turned down the bedcover and top sheet and sat on the bed.

He sat in the darkness and drank.

As the pain in his diaphragm loosened its grip, he put his glass on the bedside table and lay down.

He fell asleep almost instantly.

CHAPTER 6

Inspector Jensen woke up at half past six in the morning. He got out of bed and went to the bathroom, washed his hands and face and the back of his neck in cold water, shaved and cleaned his teeth. Once he had finished gargling, he coughed for a long time.

Then he boiled some water, stirred honey into it and tried to drink while it was as scalding hot as possible. As he did so, he read the papers. None of them said a word about the events that had kept him busy the day before.

There was heavy traffic on the motorway, and even though he used his siren it was twenty-five to nine before he walked into his office.

Ten minutes later, the chief of police rang.

'Have you started the investigation?'

'Yes.'

'Along what lines?'

'The technical evidence is being analysed. The psychologists are seeing what they can make of the wording. I've got a man working on the post office angle.'

'Any results?'

'Not yet.'

'Have you got a theory yourself?'

'No.'

Silence.

'My existing knowledge of the company in question is insufficient,' said Inspector Jensen.

'It would be a good idea to refresh it, then.'

'Yes.'

'And an even better idea to get that information from some source other than the company itself.'

'Understood.'

'I suggest the Ministry of Communications, maybe the Secretary of State for Press Affairs.'

'Understood.'

'Do you read their magazines?'

'No. But I shall now.'

'Good. And for God's sake be careful not to

annoy the publisher and his cousin.'

'Is there anything to stop me putting some of the plainclothes men on bodyguard duty?'

'For the company bosses?'

'Yes.'

'Without telling them?'

'Yes.'

'And do you consider such action justified?'

'Yes.'

'You think your people are up to a sensitive assignment like that?'

'Yes.'

The silence that followed lasted so long that Jensen's eyes drifted to the clock. He could hear the police chief breathing and tapping the table with something, presumably a pen.

'Jensen?'

'Yes?'

'From this moment on, I'm putting the investigation entirely in your hands. I don't want to be informed of your methods or any of the steps you are taking.'

'Understood.'

'The responsibility is yours. I'm relying on you.'

'Understood.'

'You're entirely clear on the general terms of reference for the investigation?'

'Yes.'

'Good luck.'

Inspector Jensen went along the corridor to the toilets, filled a paper cup with water and came back to his desk. Pulled out a drawer and took out a sachet of bicarbonate of soda, poured about three teaspoons of the white powder into the cup and stirred it with his plastic biro.

In the course of his twenty-five years of police service he had only ever seen the chief once, and had never spoken to him until the previous day. Since then they had had five conversations.

He drained the cup in a single draught, scrunched it up and threw it in the bin. Then he rang the institute of forensics. The lab technician's voice was dry and formal.

'No, no fingerprints.'

'Are you sure?'

'Of course. But for us, nothing's definitive. We'll be trying other methods of analysis.'

'The envelope?'

'One of the commonest brands. Hasn't told us much so far.'

'And the sheet of paper?'

'That, on the other hand seems to have a special structure. And it also looks as though it's been torn out of something, along one edge.'

'Will you be able to trace where from?'

'Conceivably.'

'And apart from that?'

'Nothing. We're still working on it.'

He ended the call, went over to the window and looked down into the concrete yard of

34

the police station. At the entrance to the body search area, he could see two policemen in rubber boots and waterproof overalls. They were getting hoses ready for sluicing out the arrest cells. He loosened his belt and gulped air until the gases in his stomach were forced up through his gullet.

The telephone rang. It was his man at the post office.

'This is going to take time.'

'You can have the time you need but no more.'

'How often shall I report back?'

'At eight every morning, in writing.'

Inspector Jensen replaced the receiver, put on his hat and left the room.

The Ministry of Communications was in the city centre, between the Royal Palace and the central offices of the Coalition parties. The Secretary of State for Press Affairs had his office on the second floor, with a view over the palace.

'The company is run in an exemplary fashion,' he said. 'An absolute model of free enterprise.'

'I understand.'

'What I can provide you with, however, is some purely statistical information.'

He picked up a file from his desk and flicked through it distractedly.

'They publish one hundred and forty-four different titles. Last year, the net circulation

35

of all these magazines combined amounted to twenty-one million, three hundred and twenty-six thousand, four hundred and fifty-three copies. A week.'

Jensen noted down the total on a small white card. 21,326,453.

'That is a very high figure. It means our country has the highest frequency of reading in the world.'

'Are there any other weekly magazines apart from theirs?'

'A few. They have print runs of a few thousand and are distributed only within limited areas.'

Jensen nodded.

'But the publishing company is naturally only *one* branch of the group's activities.'

'What are the others?'

'Within the remit of my department, there's a chain of printing companies mainly producing daily newspapers.'

'How many?'

'Companies? Thirty-six.'

'And how many papers?'

'A hundred or so. One moment.'

He consulted his paperwork.

'A hundred and two at present. The make-up of the newspaper chain is constantly changing. Some titles cease publication, others replace them.'

'Why?'

'In order to respond to new needs and

follow current trends.'

Jensen nodded.

'The net circulation of the daily papers last year . . .'

'Yes?'

'I've only got the figure for the country's total newspaper production. A net circulation of nine million, two hundred and sixty-five thousand, three hundred and twelve a day. It'll be about the same, anyway. There are a few newspapers printed entirely independently of the publishing group. They have big problems with their distribution, and their circulations are insignificant. If you reduce the figure I gave you by about five thousand, you should have more or less the correct number.

Jensen made another note on his slip of paper: 9,260,000. He said:

'Who controls the distribution network?'

'A democratic association of newspaper publishers.'

'All newspaper publishers?'

'Yes, with the proviso that their papers have to have print runs of more than fifty thousand.'

'Why?'

'Smaller circulation papers aren't considered profitable. In fact, the group immediately shuts down publications if their circulation falls below the figure I mentioned.'

Inspector Jensen put the slip of paper in his

pocket.

'In practice then, that means the group has control of all newspaper production in the country, doesn't it?'

'If one cares to put it that way, yes. But I would just like to point out that their titles are extremely comprehensive in their coverage, commendable in every respect. The weekly magazines in particular have proved their ability to cater for all legitimate tastes in a moderate manner. In times past, the press often exerted an inflammatory and unsettling influence on its readership. Now, its design and content are designed solely for its readers' benefit.'

He glanced into his file again and turned a page.

'. . . . and enjoyment. The publications are aimed at the family, at being something they can all read, at not creating aggression, dissatisfaction or anxiety. They satisfy ordinary people's natural need for escapism. In short, they are in the service of the Accord.'

'I understand.'

'Before the Accord came up with this definitive solution, newspaper and magazine publishing was much more fractured than it is now. The political parties and trade unions all had their own publishing arms. But as their publications gradually got into financial difficulties, they were closed down or taken

38

over by the group. Many of them were rescued thanks to . . .'

'Yes?'

'Well, thanks to the principles I have just been talking about. Thanks to their capacity for giving their readers peace of mind and security. Their capacity for being uncomplicated, easy to understand, and in tune with the tastes and concentration spans of people today.'

Jensen nodded.

'I don't think it's any exaggeration to claim that this united front on the part of the press has contributed more than anything else to consolidating the Accord. To bridging the gaps between political parties, between monarchy and republic, between the so-called upper classes and . . .'

He tailed off and looked out of the window before going on:

'It's no exaggeration, either, when they say that the credit must go to the group's management, those at the very top. Exceptional men, with great moral fibre. Completely without vanity, seeking neither titles nor power, nor . . .'

'Wealth?'

The Secretary of State turned a quick, questioning eye on the man in the visitor's armchair.

'Exactly so,' he said.

'Which other companies does the group

control?'

'I couldn't really say,' said the Secretary of State vaguely. 'Distribution companies, packaging manufacturers, shipping companies, furniture producers . . . the paper industry, of course, and it's not my department.'

He fixed Jensen with a look.

'I don't really think there's any more information of any value that I can give you,' he said. 'Incidentally, why the interest?'

'Orders,' said Jensen.

'To change the subject, what effect have the new police powers had on the figures?'

'You mean the suicide rate statistics?'

'Yes I do.'

'Positive.'

'Very pleased to hear it.'

Inspector Jensen asked four further questions.

'Doesn't the group's business activities run counter to the antitrust law?'

'I'm not a lawyer.'

'What's the group's turnover?'

'That's a technical tax matter.'

'And the owners' personal fortunes?'

'Almost impossible to estimate.'

'Have you yourself ever been employed by the group?'

'Yes.'

On the way back he stopped at a snack bar, drank a cup of tea and ate two rye rusks. As he ate, he thought about the suicide rate,

40

which had improved considerably since the imposition of the new alcohol abuse laws. The drying-out clinics didn't issue any statistics, and suicide on police property was always recorded as sudden death. Despite the very thorough body searches, these were unfortunately quite common nowadays.

By the time he got back to the Sixteenth District it was already two and the processing of the drunks was in full swing. The only reason it didn't start even earlier was that they tried to avoid making arrests before noon. It was a decision that seemed to have been arrived at for reasons of hygiene, so there would be time to disinfect the cell areas.

The police doctor stood at the duty desk smoking, with one elbow propped on the wooden counter. His coat was crumpled and bloodstained, and Inspector Jensen gave it a critical look. The other man saw it and said:

'Nothing to worry about. Just some poor bloke who . . . He's dead now. I was too late.'

Inspector Jensen nodded.

The doctor's eyelids were swollen and red-rimmed, his eyelashes caked with lumps of yellowish matter.

He gave Jensen a thoughtful look and said:

'Is it true what they say, that you've never failed to solve a case?'

'Yes,' said Jensen. 'That's right.'

CHAPTER 7

On the desk in his office lay the magazines he had asked for. One hundred and forty-four of them, stacked in four piles of thirty-six.

Inspector Jensen drank another cup of bicarbonate of soda and loosened his belt a notch further. Then he sat down at his desk and started to read.

The magazines varied somewhat in design, format and number of pages. Some of them were printed on glossy paper, others not. A comparison showed that this seemed to be the determining factor in the price.

They all had brightly coloured cover pictures, of cowboy heroes, the super-successful, members of the royal family, popular singers, famous politicians, children and animals. The children and animals were often in the same picture, in various combinations: little girls with kittens; little blond-haired boys with puppies; little boys with very big dogs; and older, almost fully grown girls with very small cats. The people in the cover pictures were attractive and blue-eyed. They had smooth, friendly faces, even the children and animals. When he got out his magnifying glass and studied the pictures more closely, he noticed that the faces had some strangely lifeless areas, as if something had been erased from the photographs; warts for example, or blackheads or bruises.

Inspector Jensen read the magazines as if they were reports, quickly but carefully, not skipping anything except what he was sure he already knew. Within an hour or so, he noticed certain elements recurred more and more frequently.

By half past eleven he had worked his way through seventy-two of the magazines, exactly half. He went down to the reception area, exchanged a few words with the officer on telephone duty, and had a cup of tea in the canteen. Despite the steel doors and solid brick walls, the sound of indignant yells and terrified howls forced its way up from the basement. As he went back to his room, he noticed that the officer in the green linen uniform was reading an issue of one of the magazines he had been studying. There were three more on the shelf under the desk.

It took him only a third of the time to go through the remaining half of the magazines. It was twenty to three as he turned the final glossy page and contemplated the last friendly face.

He ran his fingertips lightly over his cheeks and noted that the skin felt tired and slack under the stubble. He wasn't particularly sleepy and was still in sufficient pain from the tea not to want to eat.

He let himself slump a little, putting his left

43

elbow on the arm of the chair and resting his cheek in the palm of his hand as he looked through the magazines.

He had read nothing that was of any interest to him, but neither had he read anything at all that was nasty, troubling or disagreeable. Nor anything that had made him happy, angry, sad or surprised. He had accessed a series of pieces of information, mainly about cars and a variety of people in prominent positions, but none of it was of a kind that might be expected to influence anyone's behaviour or attitude. There was criticism, but it was directed almost exclusively at notorious psychopaths of history, and very occasionally at the situation in some distant country, always expressed in vague and very moderate terms.

Questions were debated, generally things that had happened in television shows, like someone swearing, or appearing with a beard or untidy hair. Stories such as these were often quite prominent, but they were always dealt with in a spirit of conciliation and understanding, clearly demonstrating that there was no call for criticism. It was an assumption that generally seemed very ready to hand.

A large part of the content was made up of fiction, presented as such, with colourful, quite lifelike illustrations. Like the factual content, the stories were always about people who achieved success, emotionally or financially. They were of different kinds, but as far as he could see, they were no more or less complicated in the big, glossy magazines than in the more comic-like publications.

It did not escape him that the magazines were aimed at different social classes, but the content remained basically the same. The same people had their praises sung; the same stories were told; and although the style varied, his concerted trawl through them left the distinct impression that everything was written by a single hand. This was naturally an absurd thought.

It also seemed absurd to imagine anyone taking exception to, or being deeply upset by, anything written in these magazines. Certainly the contributors didn't baulk at getting personal, but the splendid qualities and impeccable moral values of the personalities discussed were never questioned. Now of course it was not unthinkable that some people who had enjoyed success were left out, or not mentioned as often as others, but there was no way of establishing that, and it seemed unlikely in any case.

Inspector Jensen fished the little white card out of his breast pocket and wrote in small, neat handwriting: 144 magazines. No clues.

On the way home he felt hungry and stopped at a vending machine. He bought two plastic-wrapped sandwiches and ate them as he drove along.

By the time he got back, he already had a severe pain in the right side of his diaphragm.

He undressed in the dark and went to get the bottle and glass. He turned down the cover and sheet and sat on the bed.

CHAPTER 8

'I want a report by nine every morning. In writing. Anything they consider relevant.'

The chief of the plainclothes patrol nodded and left.

It was Wednesday and the time was two minutes past nine. Inspector Jensen went over to the window and looked down on the men in overalls, busy with their hoses and buckets of disinfectant.

He went back to his desk, sat down and read the reports. Two of them were extremely brief.

The man at the post office reported that the letter was posted in the western part of the city, no earlier than 21.00 on Sunday evening, no later than 10.00 on Monday morning.

The lab reported:

Paper analysis complete. White, wood-free paper of top quality. Place of manufacture still not known. Glue type: standard office glue, film in acetone solution. Manufacturer: indeterminable.

The psychologist:

The individual who wrote the letter can be assumed to be either of extremely rigid temperament or a very repressed character, possibly obsessive. Any flexibility in this person can be entirely ruled out. It can be assumed that the individual in question is thorough, bordering on pedantry or perfectionism, and is used to expressing him or herself, either verbally or in writing, but presumably the latter, and probably over a long period of time. Great care has been taken over the actual layout of the letter, both technically and in terms of its design and content, e.g. the choice of typeface (all the letters are of equal size) and the very even spacing. Indicates a fixed and compulsive way of thinking, as is so often the case. Some of the vocabulary choices imply that the author is a man, probably not that young, and something of an eccentric. None of these theories can be substantiated enough to be seen as definitive, but they may perhaps offer some guidance.

The report was typed in an uneven and slapdash way, with many mistakes and crossings out.

Inspector Jensen carefully put the three reports in his hole punch, made the necessary perforations in the margin and inserted them in a green file on the left-hand side of his desk.

Then he stood up, took his hat and coat and left the room.

The weather was still fine. The sunlight was sharp and white but shed no warmth; the sky was a cold blue, and despite the petrol fumes, the air felt clear and pure. On the pavements there were people who had temporarily left their cars. As ever, they were well-dressed and looked very much alike. They moved quickly and nervously, as if they couldn't wait to get back to their cars. Once inside their vehicles, their sense of integrity was intensified. Since the cars were different in size, colour, shape and horsepower, they lent their owner an identity. What was more, they brought about a sense of group identity. People with the same cars unconsciously felt that they belonged to a peer group that was easier to grasp than society under the Accord in general.

Jensen had read this in a study commissioned by the Ministry for Social Affairs. It had been carried out by some state psychologists and had circulated to the top echelons of the police. Then it had been classified.

When he was on the south side of the square, just opposite the workers' monument, he spotted a police car exactly like his own in his rearview mirror. He was pretty sure it belonged to an inspector from one of the neighbouring districts, most likely the fifteenth or seventeenth.

As he drove up to the Skyscraper he was half listening to the short-wave radio, which was issuing brief, cryptic messages at regular intervals from the radio control room to police vans and patrol cars. He knew the daily papers' police correspondents had permission to listen to all this radio traffic. Apart from road accidents, however, there was hardly ever anything sensational or exciting to be snapped up.

He drove up to the forecourt and parked in the space between the bosses' black cars and the director of publishing's white one.

A guard in a white uniform with a red peaked cap came over at once. Inspector Jensen showed his ID and went into the building.

The high-speed lift stopped automatically on the eighteenth floor and nowhere else on the way, but it was almost twenty minutes before he was admitted. He whiled away the time studying the models of the two passenger liners, named after the Prime Minister and His Majesty the King.

He was shown in by a secretary in a green suit, her eyes dull and lifeless. The room was identical to the one he had visited two days

49

before, apart from the fact that the cups and trophies in the glass-fronted cabinet were rather smaller and the view from the window was different.

The head of publishing stopped buffing his cuticles for a moment and invited him to sit down.

'Has the matter been dealt with?'

'I'm afraid not.'

'To the extent that you may require assistance or additional information, I have been asked to give you all possible assistance. I am therefore at your disposal.'

Jensen nodded.

'Though I must prepare you for the fact that I am a very busy man.'

Jensen looked at the trophies and said:

'Were you a sportsman?'

'I'm an outdoor person. Still active. Sailing, angling, archery, golf . . . Obviously not in the same class as . . .'

He gave a modest smile and gestured vaguely towards the door. A second or two later, the corners of his mouth fell again. He looked at his watch, which was large and elegant with a broad gold-link bracelet.

'How can I help you?'

Inspector Jensen had long since formulated the questions he had come to ask.

'Has anything happened that could provide a plausible explanation for the phrase "the murder committed in the building"?'

'Of course not.'

'You can't explain it, link it to anything or any person?'

'No, as I've told you, naturally I can't. The imaginings of a lunatic. A lunatic, that's the only conceivable explanation.'

'Have there been any deaths?'

'Not recently, at any rate. But on that point I recommend you ask the head of personnel. I'm really a journalist, responsible for the content and editorial layout of the magazines. And . . .'

'Yes?'

'And in any case, you're on the wrong track. Can't you see how absurd that line of reasoning is?'

'Which line of reasoning?'

The man in the silk tie looked at his visitor in confusion.

'One more question,' said Inspector Jensen. 'If we assume that the aim of the letter was harassment of the management or one of their number, in which category do you think we should be looking for the guilty party?'

'It ought to be the police's job to decide that. Anyway, I've already made my own view plain: among the mentally ill.'

'Are there no individuals or particular groups who might feasibly feel antipathy towards the group of companies or its leadership?'

'Do you know our magazines?'

51

'I've read them.'

'Then you ought to be aware that the aim of our entire policy is precisely that: not to generate antipathy, aggression or differences of opinion. Our magazines are healthy and pleasurable. The very last thing they aim to do is to complicate the readers' lives or feelings.'

The man paused briefly. Then summarised:

'The publishing house has no enemies. The same goes for its management. The very idea is absurd.'

Inspector Jensen sat upright and immobile in the visitor's chair. His face was entirely without expression.

'It's possible I may be obliged to make certain enquiries here in the building.'

'If so, your discretion must be complete,' the head of publishing responded instantly. 'Only the group chairman, the publisher and myself are aware of your task here. We will naturally do all we can to help you, but I have to emphasise one thing: it must not get out that the police are taking an interest in the company, particularly not to the employees.'

'My investigation is going to require some freedom of movement.'

The man appeared to consider this. Then he said:

'I can give you a master key and a pass granting you permission to visit the various departments.'

'Yes.'

'It would, as it were, provide a justification for your presence.'

The head of publishing drummed his fingers on the edge of the table. Then he gave a smile, secretive yet courteous, and said:

'I shall make out the pass myself; that would probably be best.'

He casually pressed a button beside the intercom, and a unit with a typewriter folded up from the side of the desk. It was a gleaming, streamlined machine, all chrome and impact-resistant enamel paint, and there was nothing to indicate it had ever been used.

The head of publishing opened a drawer and took out a small blue card. Then he swivelled the desk chair round, lightly tweaked the cuffs of his jacket, and carefully wound the piece of card into the typewriter. He took a while adjusting the settings, ran his index finger thoughtfully over the bridge of his nose, hit a few keys, pushed his glasses up on to his forehead and looked at what he had written, pulled the card out of the machine, crumpled it up, threw it into the bin and took another one out of the drawer.

He wound it in and typed slowly and painstakingly. After every keystroke, he pushed his glasses up and surveyed what he had produced.

As he crumpled up the card, his smile was no longer so courteous.

He took another one out of the drawer. The

next time, he took five.

Inspector Jensen sat straight and unmoving, and appeared to be looking straight past him, at the glass-fronted cabinet with the cups and the miniature flag.

After the seventh card, the publishing director had stopped smiling. He undid his collar and loosened his tie, took a black fountain pen with a silver monogram out of his breast pocket and began writing a draft on a sheet of white writing paper, discreetly headed with the company name.

Inspector Jensen said nothing and kept his eyes focused on the cabinet.

A drop of sweat rolled down the bridge of the head of publishing's nose and fell on to the sheet of paper.

The man appeared to give a start, and scribbled something rapidly, his pen scratching. Then he screwed up the paper in a temper and slung it under the desk. It missed the metal bin and fell at Inspector Jensen's feet.

The head of publishing got up and went over to one of the picture windows; he opened it and stood there with his back to his visitor.

Inspector Jensen looked quickly at the crumpled draft, retrieved it and put it in his pocket.

The head of publishing closed the window and came back across the room, smiling. He buttoned up his shirt, adjusted his silk tie and dispatched the typewriter with another press of the button. He put his finger on the intercom and said:

'Write out a temporary employee pass for Mr Jensen, allowing him free movement within the building. He's from the Buildings Inspection Service. Make it valid until the end of Sunday. And bring him a master key to go with it.'

His voice was hard, cold and overbearing, but his smile stayed the same.

Exactly ninety seconds later, the woman in green came in with the document and the key. The head of publishing scrutinised the pass critically and said with a slight shrug:

'All right, that'll have to do.'

The secretary's eyes wandered.

'I said that'll do,' the head of publishing said sharply. 'So you can go now.'

He scrawled a signature, handed the pass and key to his visitor and said:

'The key will admit you to all areas of potential interest. Well, not to the management's private offices, of course, nor to this one.'

'Thank you.'

'Have you any other questions? If not, then . . .'

He glanced apologetically at his watch.

'Just one detail,' said Inspector Jensen. 'What's the Special Department?'

'A project group that works on the planning

55

of new magazines.'

Inspector Jensen nodded, put the key and the blue pass in his breast pocket and left the room.

Before starting his car, he took out the crumpled sheet of paper, smoothed it out and tried the feel of it between his fingers. It seemed to be of very good quality and the size looked rather unusual.

The head of publishing's handwriting was as spiky and uneven as a child's, but not particularly hard to decipher. Jensen read:

Biulding officer hereby
Mr N. Jensen is from the inspection team within and can enter all departments exept
N. Jensen is a member of the Biulding Inspection Service and has the right to departments
Mr Jensen, bearer of this pass, is hereby entiteld to enter the company's
N. Jensen is from the inspection team and special authourity
Inspecter Inspector
Mr Jesen DAM HELL BUG

He folded up the sheet of paper and put it in the glove compartment on top of his service pistol. Then he leaned his head against the side window and looked at the Skyscraper; his gaze was unperturbed and gave nothing away.

He had a hollow feeling in his stomach. He

was hungry, but knew the pain would start as soon as he ate anything.

Inspector Jensen turned the ignition key and looked at his watch.

It was half past twelve, and already Wednesday.

CHAPTER 9

'No,' said the lab technician, 'it's not the same paper. Nor the same size. But . . .'

'But?'

'There's very little difference in the quality. The structure's similar. It's rather unique, in fact.'

'Meaning?'

'Meaning it could well be that both papers were made at the same factory.'

'I see.'

'We're just following that up. It's a distinct possibility, at any rate.'

The man seemed to be hesitating. After a moment he said:

'Is whoever wrote the sentences on this piece of paper linked to the case in any way?'

'Why do you ask?'

'A man who was here from the Institute for Forensic Psychiatry took a look at them. He concluded that the person who wrote these sentences suffers from dyslexia. He was pretty

57

certain about it.'

'Who allowed this psychiatrist to see case material?'

'I did. He's an acquaintance of mine. He happened to be here for something else.'

'I shall be reporting you for professional misconduct.'

Inspector Jensen hung up.

'Pretty certain,' he said to himself.

'Rather unique,' he said.

He went out to the toilets for a paper cup of water, put in three teaspoons of bicarbonate of soda, stirred it with his pen and drank.

He fished out the key. It was long and flat, and the complicated key-bit was a strange shape. He weighed the key in his hand and took a quick glance at the clock.

It was twenty past three, and still Wednesday.

CHAPTER 10

From the lobby of the Skyscraper, Inspector Jensen turned left and took the paternoster lift down. The stack of lift compartments sank slowly and creakily, and he kept an observant eye out to see what was on each floor as he passed it. First came a vast space in which electric trucks moved along narrow corridors between walls of brand-new, bundled magazines; then men in overalls pushing curved moulds on trolleys and the deafening racket of the rotary presses. Another floor down he saw shower rooms, toilets and changing rooms with benches and rows of green metal lockers. On the benches sat people who seemed to be on their break or had finished their shift. Most of them were leafing apathetically through colourful magazines that had presumably just come off the presses. Then his ride was at an end; he got out and was in the paper warehouse. It was quiet down there, but not entirely silent, because the collected sounds of the immense building above penetrated down as a powerful, pulsating roar. He wandered around randomly for a while in the gloom, between rows of bales and rolls of paper standing on end. The only person he saw was a pale little man in a white warehouseman's coat, who stared at him in alarm and crushed a burning cigarette in his closed hand.

Inspector Jensen left the paper store and took the lift back up. At street level he was joined by a middle-aged man in a grey suit. The man stepped into the same compartment and went with him up to the tenth floor, where they had to change. He said nothing, and did not once look at his fellow passenger. In the paternoster lift from the tenth floor, Jensen just had time to see the man in grey getting into the compartment below his own.

On the twentieth floor he changed to a third

59

paternoster lift, and four minutes later he was at the top.

He found himself in a narrow, windowless concrete corridor, which was uncarpeted. It ran in a rectangle round a core of staircases and lift systems, and around its outer sides there were white-painted doors. To the left of each door was a little plate with one, two, three or four names. The corridor was flooded with cold, blue-white light from the banks of skylights in the roof.

It was clear from the metal plates that these were the editorial offices of the comic section. He went down five flights of stairs and was still in the same section. There were very few people to be seen in the corridors, but he heard voices and the clatter of typewriters through the doors. On every floor there were noticeboards, mainly used for notices from the management to the staff. There were also time clocks, clocking in machines for the nightwatchmen and, on the ceiling, an automatic sprinkler system in case of fire.

On the twenty-fourth floor there was a total of four editorial offices. He recognised the names of the magazines and recalled that they were all of simple, basic design, their content consisting mainly of stories with gaudy illustrations.

Inspector Jensen slowly worked his way down. On every floor he did a circuit of the four corridors, two longer and two shorter, joined into a rectangle. Here, too, the doors were white and the walls bare. Apart from the names on the doors, the top seven floors were all identical. Everything was very neat and tidy; there were no signs of carelessness or neglect and the cleaning service seemed immaculate. From behind the doors, voices and ringing telephones could be heard, with the sound of a typewriter here and there.

He stopped by one of the noticeboards and read:

Do not make derogatory comments about the Publishing House or its magazines!

It is forbidden to fix pictures or objects of any kind whatsoever to the outsides of the doors!

Always act as an ambassador for the company. Even in Your time off! Remember that the Publishing House always behaves fittingly: with judgement, dignity and responsibility!

Rise above unwarranted criticism. Escapism and Dishonesty are just other names for poetry and imagination!

Always be aware that You represent the Publishing House and Your magazine! Even in Your time off!

The truest features and stories are not always the best! Truth is a commodity that needs very cautious handling in modern journalism. You cannot be sure that everyone can take as much of it as You can!

Your task is to entertain our readers, to stimulate them to dream.

Your task is not to shock, agitate or alarm, nor to rouse or educate!

There were further exhortations, all with similar content and expressed in a similar way. Most of them were signed by the company management or those responsible for the building, a few of them by the publisher himself. Inspector Jensen read them all, then continued working his way down.

The next floors he came to were evidently where the bigger, more elegant magazines were produced. They were decorated rather differently, with pale carpets in the corridors, steel chairs and chrome ashtrays. The closer he got to the eighteenth floor, the greater the cool elegance grew, only to fade away again further down. The directorate occupied four floors; below that there were offices for general administration, advertising, distribution and much more. The corridors grew bare again and the clatter of typewriters intensified. The light was cold, white and searing.

Inspector Jensen toured floor after floor. When he got down to the vast lobby, it was almost five. He had used the stairs the whole way down and felt a vague weariness in his calves and at the backs of his knees.

62

Approximately two minutes later, the man in grey came down the stairs. Inspector Jensen hadn't seen him since they parted by the paternoster lift on the tenth floor an hour earlier. The man went into the security desk at the front entrance. He could be seen saying something to the men in uniform behind the wall of glass. Then he wiped the sweat from his brow and cast a fleeting, indifferent glance round the lobby.

The clock in the big hall struck five and exactly one minute later, the automatic doors of the first fully loaded high-speed elevator opened.

The steady stream of people continued for more than half an hour before it began to thin out. Inspector Jensen, his hands clasped behind his back, stood rocking gently to and fro on the balls of his feet as he watched the people hurry past. On the far side of the revolving doors they dispersed and disappeared, timid and hunched, in the direction of their cars.

By a quarter to six, the lobby was empty. The lifts stood still. The men in the white uniforms locked the front entrance and left. Only the man in grey was left there behind the wall of glass. It was almost dark outside.

Inspector Jensen stepped into one of the aluminium-lined lifts and pressed the top button on the control panel. The lift came to a swift, stomach-lurching stop at the eighteenth floor, the doors opened and closed, and then it continued upwards.

The corridors of the comic department were still as brightly lit, but the sounds behind the doors had stopped. He stood still, listening, and after about thirty seconds he heard a lift stop somewhere nearby, presumably one floor below. He waited a bit longer but could not hear any footsteps. There was nothing to be heard at all, and yet the silence was not complete. Only when he leaned sideways and pressed his ear to the concrete wall could he make out the roar and throb of distant machine halls. When he had listened long enough, the sound became more tangible, acute and insistent like an unidentified sensation of pain.

He straightened up and walked the corridors. He was constantly aware of the sound. At the top of the last flight of stairs there were two steel doors with white enamel paint, one of them rather taller and wider than the other. Neither had a handle. He got out the key with the strangely shaped key-bit and tried it first in the smaller door, but could not get it to fit. The second door, on the other hand, opened at once and he saw a steep, narrow flight of concrete steps, sparsely lit by small white globe-shaped lights.

Inspector Jensen went up the steps, opened another door and emerged on to the roof.

It was now completely dark, and the evening

wind was chill and biting. Round the flat roof ran a brick-built parapet about a metre tall. Far below lay the town, with millions and millions of cold, white pinpricks of light. Some ten squat chimneys stuck up from the middle of the roof. Smoke was issuing from a couple of them, and despite the stiff wind he could smell the acrid, choking fumes.

He opened the door at the top of the steps and thought he heard someone shut the one at the bottom, but when he got down there, the thirtieth floor was empty, silent and deserted. He tried the master key in the lock of the smaller door one more time but still could not open it. Presumably the door led to some technical installation such as the lift machinery or the central electrical unit.

He made another circuit of the closed corridor system again, walking quietly and cautiously on his rubber soles from sheer force of habit. On the far side he stopped and listened, and again thought he could make out the sound of footsteps somewhere nearby. The sound ceased at once and might just have been an echo.

He took out the master key again, opened a door and went into one of the editorial offices. It was considerably larger than the arrest cells in the basement of the Sixteenth District police station; the concrete walls were bare and white, as was the ceiling, and the floor was pale grey. The furniture consisted of three white-painted desks, covering almost the entire floor area, and on the windowsill stood an intercom. On the desks were sheets of paper, drawings, rulers and felt pens, all tidily laid out.

Inspector Jensen paused by one of them and looked at a brightly coloured drawing, divided into four panels and clearly a comic strip. Beside the illustration lay a sheet of paper with some typed text and the heading: 'Original script from the authorial department.'

The first picture was of a restaurant scene. A blonde woman with huge breasts was sitting at a table opposite a man who had a blue mask over his eyes and was wearing a catsuit with a wide leather belt. In the middle of his chest he had a skull motif. In the background there were a dance band and people in dinner jackets and long dresses, and on the table stood a champagne bottle and two glasses. In the next picture, the man with the peculiar costume was alone; he had a glowing halo round his head and his hand was stuck in something that looked a bit like a primus stove. The next panel showed the restaurant again; the man in the catsuit seemed to be hanging in mid-air above the table, while the blonde woman looked at him expressionlessly. The last illustration was of the man in the catsuit; he was still hanging there, and the stars were visible in the background. From a ring on his right index finger sprouted a giant-sized hand on a long stalk. In the hand lay an orange.

Some parts of the picture were white: the top of the panels, and the oval shapes emerging from the gleaming teeth of the characters. In these spaces there were short, easy-to-read captions, done in capital letters in felt pen, but still not complete.

That evening, the Blue Panther and rich Beatrice meet at New York's classiest restaurant . . .
'I think . . . it feels so strange . . . I think I . . . love you.'
'What? I thought the moon just moved!'
Blue Panther sneaks out to recharge his power ring . . .
'Excuse me, but I have to leave you for a little while. There's something wrong with the moon!'
Once again the Blue Panther leaves the woman he loves to save the universe from certain destruction. It's the fiendish Krysmopomps who . . .

He recognised the characters from one of the publications he had been studying the previous evening.

Pinned to the wall above the desk was a photocopied notice. He read:

In the last quarter, circulation has risen by 26 per cent. The magazine answers a vital need and has a great task ahead of it. The bridgehead has been taken. We fight on to final victory! The Editor in Chief.

Inspector Jensen took one last look at the illustrations, switched off the light and pulled the self-locking door closed behind him.

He took the lift down eight floors and was then in the offices of one of the bigger magazines. He could now clearly hear, at regular intervals, the faint sounds made by the person who was following. So that was settled, and he didn't need to worry about it any longer.

He opened a couple of doors and went into concrete cells identical to those he had seen on the thirteenth floor. On the desks were pictures of royalty, film and pop stars, children, dogs and cats, along with articles that were obviously in the process of being translated or edited in some way. Some of them had been corrected in red ink.

He read through a few of them and found that the deletions were almost exclusively modestly critical observations or value judgements of varying kinds. The articles were about popular artistes abroad.

The editor in chief's office was larger than the rest. It had a pale beige carpet and the chairs had white PVC seat covers. On the desk, besides a loudspeaker unit, there were two white telephones, a pale grey blotter and a photograph in a steel frame. The photo was obviously of the editor in chief himself, a thin, middle-aged man with a worried expression, a doglike gaze and a well-trimmed moustache.

Inspector Jensen sat down in the chair behind the desk. When he cleared his throat, the sound echoed around the room, which seemed cold and desolate and bigger than it really was. There were no books or magazines in there, but on the white wall opposite the desk there was a big, framed picture in full colour. It was a photograph of the Skyscraper after dark, its façade illuminated by floodlights.

He opened some of the drawers but did not find anything of interest. In one of them there was a brown envelope, sealed with sticky tape and marked PRIVATE. It contained some colour photographs and a printed slip bearing the words: *This is an exclusive offer at a special reduced price from the Publishing House's international picture service, reserved for top managerial positions.* They were pictures of naked women with large, pink breasts and shaved genital areas.

Inspector Jensen carefully resealed the envelope and put it back in its place. There was no legal ban on images of that kind, but after a huge upswing in popularity a few years before, works of pornography had for some reason almost disappeared off the market. In some quarters, the slump in demand was being linked to the rapid decline in the birth rate.

He lifted the blotter and found an internal memo from the head of publishing. It read:

The piece on the wedding of the Princess and the head of the National Confederation at the Royal Palace is deplorable. A number of important people close to the Publishing House are scarcely mentioned. The hint that the groom's brother was a keen republican in his youth is downright offensive, as is the humorous remark about the possibility of the head of the National Confederation becoming King. As a professional, I also take exception to the sloppy design and layout of the feature. The reader's letter in issue 8 should never have been published. The claim that the suicide rate in the country has gone down could lead to the distressing misconception that too many people committed suicide in our Society of Accord previously. Need I point out that your circulation figures are not rising in line with management calculations?

A note in the margin indicated that the memo had been sent to all top section heads.

As Inspector Jensen re-emerged into the corridor, he thought he heard a slight rustling sound behind one of the closed doors.

He got out the master key, opened the door and went in. The lights were off, but in the faint reflection of the floodlighting he saw

70

a man slumped in a desk chair. He closed the door and switched on the light. The room was of the standard type, with concrete walls and chrome window frames. The air was heavy and suffocating, thick with the smell of alcohol, tobacco smoke and vomit.

The man in the chair appeared to be in his fifties. He was heavily built and on the plump side, and was wearing a jacket, a white shirt, a tie, shoes and socks. His trousers were spread out on the desk, where he had clearly been trying to wipe them clean; his underpants were hanging on the radiator. His chin was resting on his chest and his face was pink. On the desk stood a paper cup and an almost empty bottle of spirits, and there was an aluminium wastepaper bin between his feet.

The man grimaced at the bright, white light and stared with bloodshot eyes.

'Journalism's dead,' he said. 'I'm dead. Everything's dead.'

He groped for the bottle on the desk.

'Here I sit in this bloody soup kitchen. Hounded and ordered about by people who can't even read or write. Me! Year after year.'

He had hold of the bottle now, and poured himself the final drop.

'The biggest soup kitchen in the world,' he said. 'Three hundred and fifty portions a week. A soup made of nothing but lies, guaranteed tasteless. Year after year.'

His whole body was shaking and he needed

71

both hands to raise the cup to his lips.

'But now it's over,' he said.

He picked up a letter from the desk and waved it.

'Read this,' he said. 'Behold the finale.'

Inspector Jensen took the piece of paper. It was a communication from the editor in chief:

Your piece on the royal wedding lacks judgement, is badly written and full of errors. The publication of the reader letter on the subject of suicide in issue 8 is a scandalous lapse. I have been obliged to report the matter to the highest authority.

'He'd read the whole thing before it went for typesetting, of course. That bloody reader's letter as well. But I'm saying nothing. The poor fucker's fighting to save his own skin.'

The man regarded Jensen with fresh interest.

'Who are you? A new director? You'll be very happy here, my lad. We've got dressed-up farmhands from dunghills in the sticks as editors in chief here. And the odd village whore, of course, that somebody happens to have made a fool of himself with.'

Jensen took out his blue card. The man in the chair didn't even glance at it. He said:

'I've been a journalist for thirty years. I've seen the whole process of spiritual decay. The intellectual strangulation. The world's

72

slowest garrotte. Once upon a time, I had a will. That was wrong. I still have a bit of will, just a tiny little scrap. That's wrong, too. I can write. That's wrong. That's why they hate me. But for now, they need people like me. Until someone invents a machine that can write their bloody crap. They loathe me because I'm not an infallible machine with handles and dials that writes their crappy lies, six pages an hour, without typos or crossings-out or personal reflections. Now I'm drunk. Three cheers for that.'

His eyes were open wide and the pupils were mere dots.

'And that poor devil just hangs there like a bit of cooked macaroni,' he said.

He waved a vague hand in the direction of his penis, slumped still further and muttered:

'As soon as my trousers are dry I shall try to get myself home.'

The man sat there in silence for a while. He was breathless, his breathing uneven. He threw out his right arm and said:

'Esteemed audience! Our play is now ended and the hero will be hanged, for the human race never changes or does anything as a favour or for free. Do you know who wrote that?'

'No,' said Inspector Jensen.

He switched off the light and left the room.

On the tenth floor he transferred to the paternoster lift and took it all the way down to the paper store.

The night-time lighting was in operation, individual blue globes that shed a faint, uncertain gleam.

He stood entirely still and felt the pressure of the vast building towering above him. The rotary presses and machines had all stopped and the weight and massive solidity of the Skyscraper seemed to grow in time with the silence. He could no longer hear the sound of whoever was shadowing him.

He took the lift back up to street level. The lobby was empty and he waited. It took three minutes for the man in the grey suit to emerge from a side door and walk over to the security desk.

'There's an inebriated person in room two thousand, one hundred and forty-three,' said Inspector Jensen.

'He's being dealt with,' said the man in grey tonelessly.

Inspector Jensen opened the front entrance with his own key and stepped out into the cold night air.

CHAPTER 11

By the time he got back to the station in the Sixteenth District it was five to ten. His room offered nothing to detain him, and he went downstairs to the arrest area, where two young women were just being admitted through the entrance from the yard. He waited while they handed over their ID cards, shoes, outdoor clothes and handbags at the admittance desk. One of them swore and spat in the registering officer's face. The constable who had made the arrest yawned and twisted her wrist as he glanced wearily at his watch. The other woman under arrest just stood there, head down and arms hanging. She could not stop crying, and words came snuffling indistinctly through her tears. They were the usual ones, 'No, no,' and 'I don't want to.'

The women were bundled off by a couple of police nurses in rubber gloves and pale green plastic coats, and almost immediately there was the sound of sobbing and cries of distress as they were body-searched. The female staff were more efficient and more persistent than their male counterparts.

He went over to the admittance desk and read through the list of people booked in over the previous few hours. There had been no police intervention at the publishing house, and no reports had come from there, either.

Inspector Jensen didn't eat anything on the way home. He wasn't particularly hungry, and the hollow feeling in his stomach had faded. But despite the warmth and safety of the car, he was shivering as if he were cold, and found it hard to keep his hands still on the steering wheel.

That was the third day gone. He had four left.

CHAPTER 12

It was a cold, clear morning. There was a thin layer of fresh snow on the grass areas between the apartment blocks, and the concrete surface of the motorway had a veil of black ice.

Inspector Jensen had woken early, and despite the traffic congestion and slippery road conditions he reached his office in good time. His throat was dry, and although he had gargled and brushed his teeth, the unpleasant stale taste persisted. He sent for a bottle of mineral water from the canteen and started going through the papers on his desk. The forensics institute report hadn't arrived, and the others appeared of no interest. The man at the post office was getting nowhere. Jensen read his short account thoroughly, massaged his temples and rang the number of the main post office. It took a long time for the policeman to come to the phone.

'Jensen here.'

'Yes, Inspector.'

'What are you doing?'

'Interviewing the sorters. It's going to take quite a while.'

'Be more precise.'

'Two more days. Maybe even three.'

'Do you think it's going to give you any leads?'

'No, not really. There are lots of letters with addresses made out of bits cut from newspaper headlines. I've seen over a hundred already. Most of them aren't even anonymous. It's just something people do.'

'Why?'

'Some sort of joke, I suppose. The only employee who can remember this particular letter is the express messenger who delivered it.'

'Have you got a copy of the letter itself?'

'No, Inspector. But I've got one of the envelopes and the address.'

'I know that. Avoid giving me unnecessary information.'

'Yes, Inspector.'

'Stop what you're doing. Go to the forensics lab, have a photocopy made of the text and find out which newspapers or magazines the letters came from. Understood?'

'Understood.'

Inspector Jensen replaced the receiver. Outside the window, the sanitary squad was clattering around with its shovels and metal dustpans.

He clasped his hands and waited.

When he'd been waiting for three hours and twenty minutes, the telephone rang.

'We've identified the paper used for the letter,' said the lab assistant.

'Yes?'

'It's document-grade paper of a weight known as CB–3. It's manufactured by one of the group's own paper mills.'

The line went quiet for a moment. Then the man went on:

'Not that surprising in itself. They own practically the whole paper-making industry.'

'Get to the point,' said Inspector Jensen.

'This mill is north of here, only forty kilometres from the city. We've got a man up there. I spoke to him five minutes ago.'

'And?'

'This kind has been in production for about a year. It's mainly intended for export, but some smallish consignments have gone to a so-called job-printing firm, which also belongs to the group. They've taken delivery of two different sizes. From what I can understand, it's only the larger format that's relevant here. We won't be taking this any further now. The rest is up to your lot. I've got someone coming over with all the names and addresses. They should be with you in ten minutes.'

Jensen didn't reply.

'That's all,' said the lab assistant.

The man seemed to be hesitating. After a short, doubtful pause, he said:

78

'Er, Inspector?'

'Yes.'

'What you said yesterday, I mean about reporting me for professional misconduct. Does it still apply?'

'Of course,' said Inspector Jensen.

Ten minutes later, an officer from the uniformed branch came in with the written information.

Once Jensen had read it, he stood up and consulted the big map on the wall. Then he put on his hat and coat and went down to his car.

CHAPTER 13

The office had glass walls, and while Inspector Jensen waited for the foreman of the printing works to come back, he watched the activity on the other side, where staff in white and grey protective coats moved to and fro behind long counters. In the background he could hear the din of the typesetting machinery and printing presses.

On metal hooks along one wall of the office there were damp proofs hung up to dry. The texts, which were set in big, bold typefaces, sang the praises of the publishing house's papers and magazines. One of them imparted the news that this week one particular paper came with a fold-out poster, a life-size picture of a sixteen-year-old TV star. The poster was printed in 'glorious full colour and exceptionally beautiful'. The public was urged to buy the paper without delay, before stocks ran out.

'We do some of the company's advertising,' said the foreman. 'Those are advertisements for the daily papers. Stylish looking stuff, but very expensive. A single one of those costs as much as you or I get paid in a year.'

Inspector Jensen made no comment.

'But that's neither here nor there, of course, for the people who own the whole lot, the magazines and the daily press and the printing firms and the paper they print things on,' said the foreman.

'Elegant, no doubt about it,' he said. The man half turned away and popped a pastille in his mouth.

'You were quite right,' he said. 'We did two printing jobs on that paper. About a year back. They were really swish, too. Limited print runs. Only a couple of thousand of each. One was personal headed notepaper for the big boss, and the other one was some kind of diploma.'

'For the publishing house?'

'Yep. There ought to be sample copies here somewhere. I'll show you.'

He hunted through his files.

'Ah, here they are. Take a look.'

The chairman's notepaper was quite small in

80

format, and the discreet grey monogram in the top right-hand corner appeared to have been designed to give an impression of reticence and sober taste. Inspector Jensen saw at once that the paper size was considerably smaller than that of the anonymous letter, but he measured it anyway. Then he got out the report from the lab and compared the measurements. They didn't match.

The second piece of printed paper was a four-page booklet, almost square. The first two pages were blank, and on the third there was some text, printed in gold in big, ornamental Gothic script. It read:

IN RECOGNITION OF THE YEARS OF
FRUITFUL COLLABORATION IN
THE SERVICE OF CULTURE AND
ACCORD WE EXPRESS OUR
DEEPLY FELT THANKS.

'Nice, eh?'

'What was its intended use?'

'I don't know. Some sort of certificate. I suppose someone was going to sign it. Then they'd hand it out. That must have been what it was for.'

Inspector Jensen took his ruler and measured the front cover of the booklet. He took the card from his pocket and compared the measurements. They matched.

'Have you got any of this type of paper in

your store?'

'No, it's a special edition. Cost a small fortune, too. And the bits that were left over once we'd done the print job must have been pulped long since.'

'I'm taking this with me.'

'We've only got the one archive copy,' said the foreman.

'Oh?' said Inspector Jensen.

The foreman was a man of sixty with a lined face and melancholy look. He smelt of alcohol, printing ink and throat sweets and he didn't say a word more, not even goodbye.

Inspector Jensen rolled up the diploma and left the printing works.

CHAPTER 14

The office of the head of personnel was on the nineteenth floor. The man behind the desk was short and stout with a face like a frog, and his smile was not as well practised as the one used by the head of publishing. It just looked crooked and distorted and malicious. He said:

'Deaths? Well, there have been one or two jumpers, of course.'

'Jumpers?'

'Yes, suicides. You get a few of those everywhere, don't you?'

His observation was correct. Over the course of the previous year, two pedestrians had been killed in the city centre by falling bodies. Several more had been injured. It was one of the disadvantages of high-rise buildings.

'And apart from that?'

'Well, a few people have died in the building in recent years, always of natural causes or as the result of an accident. I'll have the administrative department send over a list.'

'Thank you.'

The head of personnel was really making an effort. He managed to make his smile look a little less off-putting and said:

'Anything else I can do for you?'

'Yes,' said Inspector Jensen, unrolling the diploma. 'What's this?'

The man looked rather taken aback.

'An address, or perhaps I should say a farewell letter, for people leaving their employment with us here. They're very costly to produce, but the intention is to give our former employees a beautiful keepsake, something to remember us by. No expense spared. That's the way the management sees it, in this as in so many other cases.'

'Are they presented to everybody when they leave?'

The man shook his head.

'No, no, of course not. That would be far too expensive. This is a mark of distinction only given to people in top posts, or colleagues in positions of particular trust. At the very least, anyone receiving it must have carried out their duties as required, and been a worthy ambassador for the company.'

'How many have been handed out?'

'Only a few. This particular kind is pretty new. We've only been using it for six months or so.'

'Where are the diplomas kept?'

'With my secretary.'

'Are they easily accessible?'

The head of personnel pressed a button on his intercom. A young woman came into the room.

'Is form PR–8 kept where outsiders could get their hands on it?'

The woman looked horrified.

'No, certainly not. It's kept in the big steel filing cabinet. I lock it every time I leave the room.'

He waved her out and said:

'She's a reliable girl, very thorough. She wouldn't be here otherwise.'

'I need a list of all the people who have received diplomas of this type.'

'Of course. That can be arranged.'

They sat in silence for quite a time, waiting while the list was drawn up. At length, Inspector Jensen asked:

'What are your main functions in this job?'

'Hiring editorial and administrative staff. And ensuring that everything possible is done to promote the well-being of the staff, and . . .'

He paused and smiled a broad smile with his frog mouth. It was hard and cold and appeared entirely genuine.

'And freeing the publishing house from those who abuse our trust,' he said. 'Dealing with staff who've neglected their duties.'

A few seconds later, he added:

'Well, it rarely comes to that, of course, and such cases are handled in the most humane way possible, like everything else here.'

Silence descended on the room again. Inspector Jensen sat entirely still, listening to the throbbing rhythm of the Skyscraper.

The secretary came in with two copies of a list. There were twelve names on it.

The head of personnel read it through.

'Two of these people have actually died since they took retirement,' he said. 'And one has moved abroad, I know that for a fact.'

He took his fountain pen from his breast pocket and put neat little ticks by three of the names. Then he passed the sheet of paper to his visitor.

Inspector Jensen glanced quickly through the list. Each name was followed by a date of birth and some brief details such as 'early retirement' or 'left at his own request'. He folded the list carefully and put it in his pocket.

Before he left, there were two more exchanges between them.

'May I ask the reason for your interest in

this particular detail?'

'An official matter that I am not at liberty to discuss.'

'Have any of our farewell letters fallen into the wrong hands?'

'I don't think so.'

There were already two men in the lift Inspector Jensen took back down. They were fairly young, and smoked cigarettes while chatting about the weather. They had a nervous, slangy, staccato way of talking that seemed to consist of a series of keywords. It was not at all easy for an outsider to understand.

When the lift stopped on the eighteenth floor, the boss, the chairman of the group, stepped in. He gave an absent nod and stood facing the wall. The two journalists extinguished their cigarettes and took off their hats.

'Just fancy it snowing,' one of them said softly.

'I feel so sorry for all the little flowers,' said the boss in his attractive, deep voice.

He said it without a single glance at the man who had spoken. He stood immobile with his face turned to the aluminium wall. Nothing more was said for the rest of the journey.

In the lobby, Inspector Jensen borrowed a telephone and rang the lab.

'Well?'

'You were right. There are traces of gold

dust. In the glue under the letters. Strange that we missed it.'

'You think so?'

CHAPTER 15

'Find out this person's address. And be quick about it.'

The head of the plainclothes patrol stood to attention and went out.

Inspector Jensen studied the list on the desk in front of him. He opened one of the drawers, got out his ruler and drew fine, straight lines through three of the names. Then he numbered the rest, from one to nine, looked at the clock and made a note in small letters at the top of the sheet: Thursday, 16.25.

He got out a fresh notebook, opened the first page and wrote: Number 1, former director of distribution, age 48, married, early retirement on health grounds.

Two minutes later the head of the plainclothes patrol was back with the address. Jensen wrote it down, shut the notebook, put it in his inside pocket and got to his feet.

'Find out the rest,' he said. 'I shall need them as soon as I get back.'

He drove through the city hub of office blocks and department stores, passed the

Trades Union Palace and joined the stream heading west. The queues of cars moved quickly along the broad, straight motorway as it cut through industrial areas and vast dormitory towns with thousands of tower blocks lined up in identical columns.

In the clear light of the evening sun, he could clearly see the pall of greyish exhaust fumes. It was about fifteen metres thick and lay like a bank of poisonous fog over the city.

Several hours earlier he had drunk two cups of tea and eaten four rusks. Now there was a pain on the right of his diaphragm, a dull, heavy ache as if a low-speed drill had been rotating in soft tissue. Despite the pain, he was still hungry.

Another ten kilometres or so further on and the tower blocks looked older and more dilapidated. They rose like pillars from vegetation that had been left untended and was now running wild; large sections of plaster had come away from the uneven, weathered blocks of lightweight concrete, and many of the windowpanes were broken. Once the authorities had found a solution to the housing problem ten years before in mass construction of a type of tower block containing only identical, standard apartments, large numbers of people had deserted the older housing areas. In most of those suburbs, only about a third of the flats were now occupied. The rest were standing empty and had been left to decay, as had the buildings as a whole. The properties were no longer profitable, so nobody bothered with their repair or upkeep. What was more, the blocks had been shoddily built and soon crumbled. Many of the neighbourhood shops had gone bankrupt and closed, or simply been abandoned by their owners, and since the state's calculations allowed for private car ownership for everyone there was no longer any public or state-owned transport serving the housing estates.

Among the scrubby trees and bushes round the blocks lay shoals of car wrecks and indestructible, throwaway plastic packaging. At the Ministry for Social Affairs they counted on the blocks gradually being abandoned entirely and falling down, at which point the areas would automatically and at no extra cost be converted into rubbish dumps.

He left the motorway, drove over a bridge and found himself on a long, leafy island dotted with swimming pools, bridleways, and white villas along the shore. He drove on for several minutes and then slowed down, turned left, through an open pair of tall wrought-iron gates, drove up to a house and stopped.

The villa was large and expensive, its spotless glass façades creating an impression of luxury. There were three cars parked beside the entrance, one of them large and silvery grey, a foreign make and the latest model.

Inspector Jensen went up the steps and as

89

he passed the electric eye a door chime rang inside the house. The door was immediately opened by a young woman in a black dress and starched, white lace cap. She asked him to wait and disappeared back into the house. The furnishing of the hall and what he could see of the other rooms was modernist and impersonal. It had the same chilly elegance as the management floors of the publishing house.

In the hall there was also a youth who looked about nineteen. He was sitting on one of the steel armchairs with his legs stretched out in front of him, staring apathetically straight ahead.

The man Jensen had come to see was a suntanned, blue-eyed individual with a thick neck, signs of encroaching corpulence, and a supercilious expression on his face. He was wearing casual trousers, sandals and a short, elegant smoking jacket of some woolly sort of fabric.

'What's this about?' he said brusquely. 'I must point out that I'm extremely short of time.'

Jensen took a step into the hall and showed his ID.

'My name's Inspector Jensen, from the Sixteenth District,' he said, 'I'm conducting an investigation that has to do with your former employment and place of work.'

The man's posture and expression changed.

He shuffled his feet uneasily and appeared to shrink. He looked scared and shifty.

'For God's sake,' he muttered, 'not here. Not here, in front of . . . Come into my . . . or the library . . . yes, the library would be better.'

He gestured vaguely, seemed to be searching for something to divert their attention, and said:

'This is my son.'

The young man in the armchair gave them a look of utter boredom.

'Aren't you going to take your new car out for a spin?' said the man in the smoking jacket.

'Why would I want to?'

'Well, girls and that sort of . . .'

'Huh,' said the youth.

His look clouded over once more.

'I don't understand young people nowadays,' the man said with an embarrassed smile.

Inspector Jensen did not respond, and the smile immediately died away.

There were no books in the library, which was a big, light room with some cupboard units and several groups of low sofas and chairs. There were magazines lying on the tables.

The man in the smoking jacket carefully closed the doors and cast an imploring look at his visitor, whose face remained grave and set. He shuddered and went over to one of the cupboards, got out a tumbler, filled it with spirits almost to the brim and drained it in a single draught. He refilled the glass, looked at Inspector Jensen again and mumbled:

'Well, it probably makes no difference now. Presumably I can't offer you . . . no, of course not . . . sorry. It's the shock, you see.'

The man collapsed on to one of the chairs. Jensen just stood there. He got out his notebook. The other man's face was already shiny with sweat. He kept mopping it with a crumpled handkerchief.

'Good God,' he said, 'I knew it. I've known it all along. That those devils would put the knife in as soon as the election was over.'

'But I shall fight it,' he said vehemently. 'They'll take the whole lot away from me, of course. But there are things I know, this and that, and they wouldn't . . .'

Jensen observed him intently.

'There are quite a few things,' the man said. 'Like figures that they'd find very hard to explain. Do you know how much income they declare for tax purposes? Do you know what their tax lawyers' salaries are? Do you know who *really* pays their tax lawyers?'

He tugged nervously at his thinning hair and said miserably:

'Sorry, sorry . . . I naturally don't mean to . . . my case can hardly be made any worse, but . . .'

His voice became suddenly insistent.

'Besides, does the interrogation have to be done here, in my own home? I assume you already know everything. Must you stand there like that? Why don't you sit down?'

Inspector Jensen stayed where he was. He still said nothing. The man drained his tumbler and set it down with a crash. His hands were shaking.

'Very well, very well, go ahead,' he said dejectedly. 'Let's get it over with. So we can get away from here.'

He stood up and went back to the cupboard, where he fumbled with the tumbler and the bottle top.

Inspector Jensen opened his notebook and got out his pen.

'When did you cease your employment?' he asked.

'Last autumn. The tenth of September. I'll never forget that day. Nor the weeks leading up to it, they were dreadful, as dreadful as this day, today.'

'You took early retirement?'

'Yes. They made me. Out of pure goodwill, of course. I even got a doctor's certificate. They thought of everything. Heart defect, they said, heart defect sounds good. There was nothing wrong with me at all, needless to say.'

'And what did your pension amount to?'

'I got full pay, and have been getting it ever since. Good God, it's peanuts to them, compared to what they have to pay their tax experts. And anyway, they could stop paying it whenever they wanted to: I'd signed the papers.'

'What papers?'

'The statement, as they called it. The confession: I assume you've read it? And the transfer of this property and my assets. They only needed them pro forma, they said, not to make use of them unless it proved necessary. Well, I've never been under any illusion, I just didn't think it would prove necessary so soon. And there were long periods when I tried to convince myself that they wouldn't report me, that they really didn't dare expose themselves to the scandal of a public trial and all the talk. They had me on a hook, after all; I mean to say, all this—' he made a sweeping gesture— 'compensates them for their losses, even if it did look a large sum.'

'How large?'

'Nearly a million. Look, must you put me through the torture of repeating this all over again? Verbally. And here . . . at home?'

'Was it all in cash?'

'No, barely half. And it was spread over many years. The rest . . .'

'Yes?'

'The rest was materials, mostly building materials, transport, labour, paper, envelopes. He had it all on his list down to the last paper clip and rubber band and pot of glue, the devil.'

'Who?'

'That devil in charge of their investigation. Their favourite Rottweiler, the head of publishing. I didn't see them in person, not even once. They didn't want to dirty their hands with a thing like that, he said. And nobody was to know anything about it. It would do irreparable damage to the group, he said. There was an election coming up straight afterwards. I suspected they'd just wait until it was over.'

He was constantly mopping his face with his handkerchief, which was already grey and sodden.

'What . . . What are you going to do with me?'

'When you stopped work, were you given some kind of diploma, a farewell letter?'

The man in the smoking jacket shuddered.

'Yes,' he said flatly.

'Please show it to me.'

'Now?'

'Yes, at once.'

The man got unsteadily to his feet, tried to adjust his expression, and went out of the room. A few minutes later he was back with the diploma. It was under glass in a frame with a broad gold edge. The message was signed by the chairman and the publisher.

'There were two more sheets to it, a pair of blank pages. What have you done with them?'

The man regarded Jensen in bewilderment.

'Don't know. Threw them away, I suppose. I think I cut that bit off before I went to the framing shop.'

'You don't remember for sure?'

'No, but I must have thrown them away. I remember cutting them off.'

'With scissors?'

'Er, yes, I'm sure of it.'

He stared at the frame and shook it.

'What a charade,' he muttered. 'What hypocrisy, what bloody hypocrisy.'

'Yes,' said Inspector Jensen.

He closed his notebook, put it in his pocket and got up.

'Goodbye,' he said.

The man stared at him uncomprehendingly. 'When . . . when are you coming back?'

'Don't know,' said Inspector Jensen.

The youth in the hall was still sitting in the same position, but was now studying the horoscope in one of the magazines with a faint glimmer of interest.

It was already dark by the time Inspector Jensen drove back, and in the decaying dormitory towns, the tower blocks were massed like queues of black ghosts in the scrubby woodland.

He didn't bother to go to the office but drove straight home. On the way he stopped at a snack bar. Though he was well aware of the consequences, he had three sandwiches and two cups of black coffee.

That was the fourth day gone.

CHAPTER 16

The phone rang before Inspector Jensen was dressed. It was five to seven in the morning and he was standing in front of the bathroom mirror, shaving. During the night he had been afflicted by severe colic; the griping pain had subsided but his midriff still felt tender and bruised.

He knew it must be to do with work, because he never used the phone for private calls and did not let anyone else do so, either.

'Jensen,' said the police chief, 'what in the name of God are you playing at?'

'We've still got three days at our disposal.'

'That's not precisely what I meant.'

'I've only just started the interviews.'

'I wasn't referring to the pace, Jensen.'

There was no answer to that. The police chief gave a gravelly cough.

'Luckily enough, for you and for me, the matter's already been cleared up.'

'Cleared up?'

'Yes, they've found out who did it.'

'Who are "they"?'

'The group's own people. As we assumed from the word go, it was a misguided prank. One of the employees, a journalist on one of the papers. Apparently a rather bohemian young man with lots of wild ideas, but a good

97

boy at heart. They seem to have suspected him all along, though they didn't bother to say so.'

'I see.'

'I assume they didn't want to cast suspicions until they had some evidence.'

'I see.'

'Anyway, it's all settled. They're dropping the charge. Taking the financial loss and tempering justice with mercy. The only thing you need to do is go and formally accept his confession. Then you can close the case.'

'I see.'

'I've got the man's address here, can you take it down?'

Inspector Jensen wrote the information on the back of a little white card.

'It's probably best for all parties if you go round there as soon as possible. So we can get this all over and done with.'

'Yes.'

'Tidy up the loose ends in the usual way and then make a copy of the paperwork. Just in case they want to see how the case was handled.'

'I see.'

'Jensen?'

'Yes.'

'No need for you to feel deflated. It's only natural for things to turn out this way. Of course the group's own people had better prospects of solving the case quickly. Their knowledge of their staff and the internal situation gave them a big head start.'

Inspector Jensen said nothing. The police chief's breathing was heavy and uneven.

'There's one other thing,' he said.

'Yes.'

'I indicated from the outset that you were to focus entirely on the investigation of the threatening letter, didn't I?'

'Yes, that's right.'

'That means you need not and ought not to take account of any other matters that have emerged during the investigation. As soon as this young joker's confession has been verified and dealt with, you are to put the matter aside. You're free to forget the whole affair. Understood?'

'Understood.'

'I think that will be the best thing for all concerned and as I said, not least for you and me.'

'I see.'

'Excellent. Goodbye.'

Inspector Jensen returned to the bathroom and finished shaving. Then he got dressed, drank a cup of hot water and honey and read the newspaper, taking his time.

Although the traffic was less dense than usual, he kept to a moderate speed on the motorway, and when he parked outside the station it was already half past nine.

He sat at his desk for a while, not bothering with the reports or the pre-prepared

99

address list. Then he rang for the man in the plainclothes patrol, gave him the white card and said:

'Find out what you can about this individual. Everything you can get hold of. And be quick about it.'

He stood at the window for a long time, watching the sanitary squad, who had still not completed their disinfection when two police officers in green uniforms dragged in the first blind drunk arrest of the day. A while later, the man who had been making investigations at the post office rang.

'Where are you?'

'In the central newspaper archive.'

'Any results to report?'

'Not yet. Shall I carry on?'

'Yes,' said Inspector Jensen.

The head of the plainclothes patrol returned just over an hour later.

'Well?'

'Age twenty-six. Son of a well-known businessman. The family's thought to be wealthy. Occasionally works as a journalist on a weekly magazine. Well educated. Unmarried. Seen as enjoying the protection of his bosses, apparently because of family connections. Temperament . . .'

The police officer frowned and studied the sheet of paper as if finding it hard to decipher his own handwriting.

'Unstable, spontaneous, charming, sense

of humour. Given to reckless pranks. Poor nerves, not very reliable, lacks stamina. Seven convictions for drunkenness, two periods of treatment in the alcohol addiction clinic. Sounds like the black sheep of the family,' concluded the head of the plainclothes patrol.

'That will do,' said Inspector Jensen.

At half past twelve he had lunch sent up from the canteen: two soft-boiled eggs, a cup of tea and three wheaten rusks.

When he had finished his meal he stood up, put on his hat and coat, went down to the car and drove south.

He found the address he had been given on the second floor of an ordinary block of flats, but no one answered when he rang the bell. He listened, and thought he could make out a vague musical sound from inside the flat. After a minute or two, he tried the handle. The door was unlocked and he went in.

It was a standard flat with a hall, kitchen and two other rooms. The walls in the first room were bare and there were no curtains at the windows. In the middle of the floor stood a wooden chair, and beside it an empty cognac bottle. On the chair sat a naked male figure, playing the guitar.

He put his head on one side and surveyed his visitor, but did not stop playing or say anything.

Inspector Jensen went on into the next room. That had no proper furniture either,

101

and no carpet or curtains, but on the floor there were some bottles and a heap of clothes. On a mattress in one corner a woman was asleep in a tangle of sheets and blankets with her head buried in a pillow. She had one arm resting on the floor, where cigarettes, a brown PVC bag and an ashtray were within easy reach.

The air was thick and stale, smelling of alcohol, tobacco smoke and naked human bodies. Inspector Jensen opened the window.

The woman lifted her head from the pillow and gave him a blank stare.

'Who the hell are you?' she said. 'What are you doing here?'

'It's the detective we've been waiting for all day, darling,' called the guitar player from the outer room. 'The great detective who's come to expose us.'

'Go to hell,' said the woman, her head sinking back on to the pillow.

Jensen went over to the mattress.

'Show me your ID card,' he said.

'Go to hell,' she said in a muffled, sleepy voice.

He bent down, opened her handbag and rummaged around until he found the card. He glanced through the personal details. She was nineteen. In the top right-hand corner there were two red marks, fully visible even though someone had tried to blot them out. That meant two arrests for drinking. A third would

102

mean immediate admittance to an alcohol abuse clinic.

Inspector Jensen left the flat. He stopped at the door and turned to the guitar player.

'I'll be back in five minutes. Make sure you're dressed.'

He went down to the car and called for an emergency vehicle. It arrived within three minutes, and he took two constables with him up to the flat. The guitar man had put on a shirt and trousers and was sitting on the windowsill, smoking. The woman was still asleep.

One of the constables produced a breath test kit, raised her head from the pillow and put the mouthpiece between her lips.

'Breathe out,' he said.

The crystals in the rubber bag turned green.

'Put your clothes on,' said the policeman.

The woman was awake at once. She sat up from the tangle of bedclothes and pulled one of the sheets over her breasts with clumsy, trembling hands.

'No,' she said. 'No, you can't. I haven't done anything. I live here. You can't. No, no, for God's sake, no.'

'Get dressed,' said the constable with the breath test, pushing the pile of clothes towards her with his foot.

'No, I don't want to,' she shouted, throwing the clothes across the floor.

'Take her in the blanket,' said Inspector

103

Jensen. 'And be quick about it.'

She stared at him in wild, wordless horror. The right side of her face was a streaky red from the pressure of the pillow and her short, dark hair was a tangled mess.

Inspector Jensen went into the other room. The man was still sitting on the windowsill. The woman was crying, shrilly and hysterically, and seemed to be putting up a fight, but it didn't last long. Within two minutes the policemen had overpowered her and taken her away. Jensen checked the time on his watch.

'Was that really necessary?' said the man at the window.

His voice was cultivated but uncertain, and his hands were shaking.

'So it was you who sent the letter?' said Inspector Jensen.

'Yes, I admit it. I already bloody have.'

'When did you send it?'

'On Sunday.'

'What time?'

'In the evening. I don't remember what time.'

'Before or after nine o'clock?'

'After, I think. I don't remember the time, I told you.'

'Where did you put the letter together?'

'At home.'

'Here?'

'No, at my parents'.'

104

'What sort of paper did you use?'

'An ordinary bit of white paper.'

His confidence was growing and he regarded Jensen coldly.

'Typewriter paper?'

'No, a thicker kind. A bit off some kind of diploma.'

'Where did you get this paper?'

'At the publishing house. It was just lying around. People who leave or get the sack get given that sort of thing, I think. Do you want me to describe it?'

'No need. Where did you find it?'

'I told you: at the publishing house.'

'Be more specific.'

'It was just lying around. Someone must've had it as a sample, I guess.'

'Did you find it on a desk?'

'I think so.'

He seemed to be considering.

'Or it could have been on some shelf.'

'When was this?'

'Oh, a few months ago. Whether you believe it or not, I can't recall exactly. No, I really can't remember, but it wasn't this year at any rate.'

'So you took it with you?'

'Yes.'

'As a joke?'

'No, I thought I might use it for some shenanigans later on.'

'Shenanigans?'

'A stunt, if you like.'

105

'What sort of stunt?'

'Oh, there are lots of uses for a diploma like that. Sign it with a false name, stick a naked woman on the front and send it to some idiot.'

'When did you get the idea for the letter?'

'Last Sunday. I was just hanging around. And then it came to me that there was a way of putting the wind up that lot for a while. It was just a joke, of course. I didn't think they'd take it that seriously.'

He had spoken with growing assurance and lucidity. Now he said, in a tone of appeal:

'I mean, I wasn't to know they'd kick up such a hell of a fuss. Didn't think it through.'

'What sort of glue did you use?'

'Some I had. Just ordinary glue.'

Inspector Jensen nodded.

'Show me your ID card.'

The man produced his card at once. It had six red marks, all crossed through in blue.

'There's no point taking me in for being drunk, I've got three in hand.'

Jensen gave back the card.

'She hasn't,' said the man, nodding towards the other room. 'And anyway, it was your fault in a way. We've been waiting for you since some time last night, and what're we supposed to do in the meantime? I can't bear sitting still. Poor kid.'

'Is the woman your fiancée?'

'Yes, I suppose you could put it like that.'

'Does she live here?'

'Yes, usually. She's fine, a nice sort of girl, but hard work. A bit old fashioned. She's really into me, if you know what I mean, Inspector.'

Jensen nodded.

'Can I just ask, if my uncle . . . if that lot up there hadn't been decent enough to drop the charge, what sort of sentence would I have got?'

'That would have been up to the court,' said Jensen.

He closed his notebook.

The man got out a cigarette and lit it. He had jumped down from the windowsill and was leaning casually against the wall.

'The bloody stupid things you find yourself doing,' he said. 'Thank God I was born lucky.'

Jensen put his notebook away in his pocket and glanced towards the door.

'The letters you used for the message, you tore them out of the paper, didn't you?'

'I certainly did.'

'You tore them?'

'Yes.'

'You didn't cut them out? With scissors?'

The man put a hand to the bridge of his nose. Smoothed his eyebrows with his fingers and frowned. Then he looked at Jensen.

'I can't really be sure,' he said at last.

'Try.'

Pause.

'No, I can't remember.'

'Where did you post the letter?'

'Here. In town.'

'Be more precise.'

'In a postbox somewhere.'

'Tell me exactly where the postbox was.'

'I can't, actually.'

'You don't know where you posted the letter?'

'Yes, I told you, it was somewhere in town. But I don't remember exactly where.'

'Don't you?'

'No, it would be absurd to expect me to. The place is full of postboxes, isn't it?'

Jensen didn't reply.

'Isn't it?' the man said irritably.

'Yes, that's right.'

'Well then.'

'But you remember which part of the city you posted it in, at any rate?'

Jensen looked out of the window, expressionless.

The other man was trying to catch his eye. When that failed, he looked away and said:

'No, I don't remember. Does it matter?'

'Where do your parents live?'

'Over to the east.'

'Perhaps you posted the letter near where they live?'

'I tell you I don't know. Why the hell does it matter?'

'Didn't you in fact post the letter here in the south?'

'Of course I bloody did. No, hang on, I don't

know.'

'Where did you post the letter?'

'I don't know, for God's sake, I've told you that,' the man said hysterically. He was breathing heavily. After a moment's pause he said:

'I drove round the whole town that evening.'

'Alone?'

'Yes.'

'And you don't know where you posted the letter?'

'No, how many times have I got to repeat myself?'

He started walking to and fro across the floor, taking small, restless steps.

'So you don't remember?'

'No.'

'You don't know where you posted the letter?'

'No,' shouted the young man, unable to control himself.

'Get your coat on and come with me,' said Inspector Jensen.

'Where to?'

'To the Sixteenth District police station.'

'Can't I just pop in and sign the papers tomorrow? I've got . . . other things to do tonight.'

'No.'

'And if I refuse?'

'It's not within your right to refuse. You're under arrest.'

'Under arrest? What the hell do you mean, you stupid flatfoot? They've dropped the charges, haven't they? Under arrest? What for?'

'For giving false or misleading evidence.'

Not a word was said in the car. The man under arrest sat in the back seat and Jensen could see him in the rearview mirror, almost without moving his eyes. The man looked nervous. He was continually blinking behind his glasses, and when he thought he wasn't being watched he bit his nails.

Jensen drove into the yard and parked by the entrance to the arrest area. He walked his charge past the inspection desk, along the row of cells where drunks were sobbing or slumped hopelessly on their benches behind the gleaming steel bars, and opened a door. The room inside was brightly lit. The ceiling, walls and floor were white, and in the middle of the room was a stool with a white seat of hard plastic.

The man looked around, defiant but at a loss, and sat down on the stool. Inspector Jensen left him there, turning the key on the outside of the door.

Up in his office he lifted the telephone receiver, dialled three digits and said:

'Send an interrogator to the solitary confinement cell. A false confession that needs retracting. And be quick about it.'

Then he took a white card out of his breast

pocket, laid it on the desk and drew a tiny, five-pointed star in the top left corner. He slowly and carefully filled the entire width of the card with stars just like it. In the next row he drew six-pointed stars, all identical and very small, and then repeated the row of five-pointed stars. Once he had reached the bottom row, he counted up the stars. Altogether he had drawn 1,242 stars, 633 with five points and 609 with six.

He had heartburn and a churning in the pit of his stomach, and it was getting on his nerves, so he drank a cup of bicarbonate of soda. From the yard came yells and other noise to indicate some kind of violent scuffle, but he didn't bother to go over to the window.

Four hours and twenty-five minutes passed, and then the telephone rang.

'That's done,' said the interrogator. 'It wasn't him, but we had to dig deep.'

'And the report?'

'Signed and ready.'

'The motive?'

'Money, I should think. He's still refusing to admit it, of course.'

'Let him go.'

'Are we proceeding to a prosecution?'

'No.'

'Do you want me to get out of him who paid him?'

'No.'

'It would be easy, now.'

111

'No,' said Inspector Jensen, 'There's no need.'

He put down the receiver. He ripped up the card covered in stars and threw the pieces in the bin. Then he picked up the list of nine numbered names, turned to a new page in his notebook and wrote: Number 2. Age 42, reporter, divorced, left at his own request.

Inspector Jensen drove home and went to bed without eating or drinking anything. He was very tired and the heartburn had gone, but it took him a long time to get to sleep.

That was the fifth day, and it had been a complete waste of time.

CHAPTER 17

'It was the wrong man,' said Inspector Jensen.

'I don't understand. What happened? He owned up, didn't he?'

'His confession was a work of fiction.'

'And he admitted that?'

'Yes, eventually.'

'So you're telling me the man confessed to something he didn't do? Are you sure?'

'Yes.'

'Did you get to the bottom of what made him do that?'

'No.'

'Doesn't that detail have implications for

the rest of the investigation?'

'Not necessarily.'

'No, maybe that's best,' said the police chief.

He sounded as though he was talking to himself.

'Jensen?'

'Yes.'

'You're in a rather unenviable situation at the moment. As far as I'm aware, they still want the perpetrator caught. You have a bare two days left. Will you pull it off?'

'I don't know.'

'If you haven't managed to lay hands on whoever did it by Monday, I can't answer for the consequences. In fact I can't even imagine them. Need I spell that out?'

'No.'

'Our failure could create unpleasantness for me personally.'

'Understood.'

'After this unexpected turn of events it's naturally more vital than ever for the investigation to be carried out with the utmost discretion.'

'Understood.'

'I'm relying on your judgement. Good luck.'

The police chief had rung at almost exactly the same time as the morning before, but this time Jensen was on his way out when the call came through. He had only had two hours' sleep the previous night, but still felt refreshed and fairly well rested. The honey water had not

113

satisfied his hunger, however, and the hollow feeling in his diaphragm showed no sign of abating.

'I shall have to eat a cooked meal soon. Tomorrow, or the day after at the latest.'

He said this to himself as he went down the stairs. It was very rare for him to talk to himself.

Light rain towards morning had dissolved the covering of snow. The temperature was now a degree or so above freezing, the clouds had dispersed and the sunlight was white and cold.

In the station in the Sixteenth District they still hadn't completed the early-morning chores. Outside the entrance to the arrest area stood the metallic grey van that was to take those who were on their third arrest for drinking to clinics and work camps, and down in the basement the staff were just bundling their dishevelled charges out of the cells. The officers looked washed out by night duty and exhaustion. At the door, those who had been released waited in a long, silent queue to file past the inspection desk and be given their pre-discharge injections.

Inspector Jensen stopped at the doctor's desk.

'What sort of night's it been?'

'Normal. That's to say, a bit worse than the night before.'

Jensen nodded.

'We had another sudden death last night, a woman.'

'Oh yes?'

'She even told us in advance. Said she'd only been drinking to get her courage up, and the police had interrupted her. And even so I wasn't able to stop her.'

'What did she do?'

'Threw herself against the cell wall and smashed her skull. Pretty difficult to achieve, but plainly it is possible.'

The doctor looked at Jensen. His eyes were puffy and red-rimmed, and there was a faint smell of alcohol that did not seem to be coming from the man he was just injecting.

'That takes strength and a heck of a lot of willpower,' said the doctor. 'And you have to tear the soundproof padding off the wall first.'

Most of those who had just been released were standing there with hands in pockets and heads hanging apathetically. There was no terror or despair in their faces any longer, just emptiness.

Inspector Jensen went up to his office, got out one of his cards and made two notes.

Better wall padding.

New doctor.

The room held nothing of interest for him this time, either, and he left it almost immediately.

It was twenty past eight.

115

CHAPTER 18

The suburb was twenty kilometres or so south of the city, and in the category the experts at the Ministry for Social Affairs liked to call 'self-clearance areas'.

It had been built at the time of the big housing shortage and consisted of about thirty tower blocks, ranged symmetrically round a bus station and a so-called shopping centre. The bus route had been axed and nearly all the shops were boarded up. The big, paved piazza was used as a car graveyard, and only about twenty per cent of the flats in the tower blocks were occupied.

Inspector Jensen located the address he was looking for with some difficulty, parked the car and got out. The block of flats was fourteen storeys high, and in the places where the plaster had peeled away the walls were black with damp. The paving in front of the main entrance was strewn with broken glass, and the vegetation of scrubby trees and bushes had pushed its way right up to the concrete base of the building. Their roots would eventually undermine the foundations.

The lift wasn't working and he had to walk up to the ninth floor. The stairwell was cold and dirty and badly lit. Some of the doors were open, revealing rooms just as people had left them, littered and draughty, with long cracks in ceilings and walls. It was apparent from the smell of frying food and the boom of presenters' voices from morning TV programmes that some of the flats were still lived in. The walls and double floors seemed to have no soundproofing effect at all.

Inspector Jensen was breathing quite heavily after five sets of stairs, and by the time he got right up to the flat his chest was tight and the right side of his diaphragm ached badly. After a few minutes, his breathing was more regular again. He took out his police ID and knocked at the door.

The man opened it at once. He said:

'Police? I'm teetotal, have been for years.'

'Inspector Jensen from the Sixteenth District. I'm conducting an investigation that has to do with your former employment and place of work.'

'Yes?'

'A few questions.'

The man shrugged. He was well dressed, and had a thin face and a resigned look in his eyes.

'Come in,' he said.

The flat was of the standard type, as were the furnishings. There was a shelf with about ten books on it, and on the table were a cup of coffee, some bread, butter and cheese and a magazine.

'Please have a seat.'

117

Jensen looked about him. The flat resembled his own in all the essentials. He sat down and got out his pen and notepad.

'When did you cease your employment?'

'Last December, just before Christmas.'

'You handed in your notice?'

'Yes.'

'Had you worked for the group for long?'

'Yes.'

'Why did you leave?'

The man drank some of his coffee. Then he looked at the ceiling.

'It's a long story. I scarcely think it can be of any interest to you.'

'Why did you leave?'

'Okay, I'm not hiding anything, but it's a bit hard to explain how it all happened.'

'Try.'

'To start with, the statement that I left of my own volition is a modification of the truth.'

'Explain.'

'It would take days, and you still might not understand. I can only give you a summary of the actual chain of events.'

He paused.

'But first I want to know why. Am I suspected of anything?'

'Yes.'

'You won't say what, I take it?'

'No.'

The man stood up and went over to the window.

118

'I came here when all these flats were newly built,' he said. 'It's not that long ago. Just after that I was taken on by the group, more or less by unhappy accident.'

'Unhappy accident?'

'I worked for another paper before; I don't suppose you remember it. It was run by the socialist party and the trade union movement, and it was the last weekly of any size left in the country that was independent of the group. It had certain ambitions, not least in the cultural sphere, though the climate on that front was getting difficult even then.'

'Cultural ambitions?'

'Yes, it made the case for good art and poetry, printed short literary fiction and so on. I'm no expert on that side of things; I was a reporter, dealing with social and political issues.'

'Were you a socialist?'

'I was a radical. In fact, I was on the extreme left wing of the socialist party, though I didn't realise it myself.'

'What happened?'

'The paper wasn't doing spectacularly. It didn't make much profit, but it didn't make a loss either. A fair number of people read it and depended on it. It was the only real counterweight to the group's papers, and it opposed the group and the publishing house and criticised them, sometimes actively, and sometimes by its mere existence.'

'How?'

'Through polemic, leaders, open criticism. By dealing with various issues honestly. That lot in the Skyscraper hated it of course, and hit back in their own way.'

'How?'

'By publishing more, and ever more trivial, comics and story magazines; by exploiting people's general tendency.'

'And what's that?'

'To like looking at pictures better than reading, and if they read anything at all to prefer meaningless drivel to things that force them to think or make an effort or take a stance. That's how it was even then, I'm afraid.'

He stayed at the window, his back to his visitor.

'The phenomenon was known as intellectual laziness and was one of the temporary unhealthy consequences of the TV age, it was said.'

A jet plane roared over the house in the direction of an airport many kilometres further south. From it, large groups of people were daily flown abroad to spend their annual weeks of recreation at a few chosen destinations where conditions were suitable. The operation was organised to the very limits of what was feasible. Jensen had once been on a trip of that kind, and he did not intend to repeat the experience.

'Back then, a lot of people still thought the rising levels of impotence and frigidity were the result of radioactive fallout. Do you remember?'

'Yes.'

'Well, the Skyscraper group couldn't get at our readership. It wasn't that large but it was consolidated, made up of people who really needed the paper. For them it was the last breathing hole in the sugar glaze. I think that was the main reason the publishing house always loathed us. But they couldn't break us, we thought.'

He turned round and looked at Jensen.

'I'll have to compress everything. I did say it couldn't all be explained in a couple of minutes.'

'Go on. What happened?'

The man gave a wan smile and went back to the sofa, where he sat down.

'What happened? The most sordid thing imaginable. They bought us, it was as simple as that. Lock, stock and barrel: our staff and our ideology and the whole damn lot. For money. Or to put it another way: the party and the trade union movement sold us, to the opposing camp.'

'Why?'

'That's not easy to explain, either. We were at a crossroads. The Accord was starting to take shape. It's a long time ago now. Do you know what I think?'

'No.'

'That it was just about the time when socialism in other countries had got over its long crisis and succeeded in consolidating people, as people I mean, made them freer, more secure, spiritually stronger, taught them what work can and should imply, set their personalities in action, inspired them to take responsibility. For our part, we were still ahead in materialist terms, so that should have been the moment for implementing others' best practice. But something entirely different happened. Things developed along a different course. Are you finding this hard to follow?'

'Not at all.'

'Here, we were so dazzled by our own superiority, so full of blind faith in the results of what was called practical politics, to put it crudely, we thought we'd managed to reconcile, virtually fuse, Marxism with plutocracy and that socialism would make itself redundant, something that reactionary theoreticians had in fact predicted years before. And that was when they started changing the party programme. They simply ditched the sections that were seen as a threat to the Accord. Step by step, they backed away from nearly all their central principles. And at the same time, in the wake of all this general mumble, the moral reactionaries broke through. You see what I'm driving at?'

'Not yet.'

122

'What they were attempting to do was to bring all the different points of view closer to each other. Perhaps it wasn't such a bad notion, but the methods that were being used to realise it were built almost entirely on hushing up any antagonism and difficulty. They lied away the problems. They glossed over them with constant improvements in material standards, and hid them behind a fog of meaningless talk pumped out via the radio, press and TV. And the phrase that covered it all was, then as now, "harmless entertainment". The idea was, of course, that the contained infections would heal themselves over time. It didn't happen. The individual felt physically looked after but robbed of his spiritual autonomy; politics and society became diffuse and incomprehensible; everything was acceptable but nothing was interesting. The individual reacted with bewilderment and gradually growing indifference. And at the bottom of it all there was this indefinable terror.

'Terror,' the man went on. 'I don't know what of. Do you?'

Jensen looked at him without expression.

'Maybe simply of living, as always. The absurd thing was, superficially everything just went on getting better. There were only three blots in the copybook: alcoholism, the suicide rate and the downward curve on the birth-rate graph. It wasn't considered proper to mention those, and it still isn't.'

He fell silent. Inspector Jensen said nothing.

'One piece of Accord reasoning that permeated everything, even if it was never said aloud or put down in writing, was that everything had to make a profit. And the remarkable thing was that this very doctrine was the fundamental reason for the trade union movement and the party selling us to what we perceived at the time as the arch-enemy. So the motive was simply money, not that they wanted to be rid of our outspokenness and radicalism. That was a bonus they only discovered later.'

'And that made you bitter?'

The man did not seem to catch the question.

'But that wasn't the most excruciating and humiliating thing about it all. Even worse was the fact that it was all done without our knowledge, at a level high above our heads. I suppose we'd imagined we were of some significance, and what we said and what we represented and the group we represented meant at least something, at least enough for us to be considered worth telling about their plans for us. But no. The whole thing was settled in private between the chairman of the group and the leader of the union movement, by two businessmen at a conference table. Then the Prime Minister was informed, and the party, which sorted out some of the practical details. Those among us who were better known or in leading positions were shoved away into sinecures in the administration, and the rest of us went, too, as part of the deal. Well, the least important ones got the sack, of course. I was in the middle category. That was what happened, that time. It could just as well have been the Middle Ages. Because that's the way it's been done, through the centuries. And it showed us, the ones who worked there, that we meant nothing and couldn't do a thing. That was the worst thing. It was murder. The murder of an idea.'

'And that made you bitter?'

'More like resigned.'

'But you felt hatred for your new workplace? For the group and its management?'

'No, not at all. If you think that, you've misunderstood me. They'd only acted entirely logically, from their own point of departure. Why should they forgo such an easy triumph? Imagine if General Miaja had rung Franco during the siege of Madrid and said, "Would you like to buy my planes? They use too much fuel." Does that analogy help you at all?'

'No.'

'It's not really adequate, anyway. Well, I can give you an unambiguous answer to your question, at any rate. No, I didn't feel hatred for the publishing house, not then, and nor did I later. I was well treated there.'

'But they fired you?'

125

'Humanely, mark you. And I brought it on myself.'

'How?'

'I deliberately abused their trust: that's the phrase.'

'In what way?'

'I was sent abroad last autumn to gather material for a series of articles. They were going to be about a life, one man's route to riches and success. The man in question was an internationally famous TV star, the kind the people are continually force-fed with. That was what they kept me busy with all these years, writing rose-tinted, doctored biographies of famous people. But that was the first time they sent me to another country to do it.'

He smiled his wan smile and drummed his fingers on the edge of the table.

'This man, this celebrity, happened to have been born in a socialist country, one of the most studiously overlooked, in fact. I don't think our government has acknowledged its existence.'

He gave Inspector Jensen a sad, searching look.

'Do you know what I did? I used the assignment as the basis for a detailed and largely positive analysis of the political and cultural standards of that country, compared to ours. The articles weren't published, of course, and I hadn't expected them to be.'

He paused briefly and frowned. Then he said:

'The funny thing is, I still don't know why I did it.'

'Bravado?'

'That's not inconceivable. But still, I haven't spoken about all these things for many years. I don't know why I'm doing it now, in fact. I don't think they've even crossed my mind. I lost heart within a couple of weeks of starting at the publishing house, and then I just sat there writing what they wanted, page after page of it. At the beginning they were obviously more worried about me than they needed to be. Then they realised I wasn't a threat and could be turned into a useful little cog in the big machine. But to start with there was talk of transferring me to the Special Department. Maybe you don't know what they do there?'

'I've heard it mentioned.'

'It's also called Department 31. It's viewed as one of the most important. I don't know why. You seldom hear anything about it; its work is kept very hush-hush. I'm pretty sure it works on projections of some kind: a dummy group is the slang term for it, in the profession. A move there was on the cards for me at one stage, but then I suppose they saw that all I was fit for was fabricating nice, pretty life stories for well-known people. And they were right.'

He fiddled absentmindedly with his coffee cup.

'Then all of a sudden I went and did that. My God, it caught them on the hop.'

Inspector Jensen nodded.

'You see, I'd realised I wouldn't ever write any more, and it dawned on me that I couldn't bear the last thing I wrote to be some rose-tinted, tear-jerking pack of lies about that lout, a piece of flattery for a clown who earns millions from looking gross and not being able to sing, and who goes round the world causing scandals in gay brothels.'

'The last thing you wrote?'

'Yes, I've stopped. I'd known for a while that I'd written all I was going to and wouldn't be able to produce any more. Eventually I'm going to find some entirely different line of work, anything at all. It might not be very easy, because we journalists don't really know how to do anything. But it'll be okay; these days, nobody needs to know how to do anything.'

'What do you live on?'

'The publishing house treated me very kindly. They said they knew I was burnt out, gave me four months' salary and let me go straight away.'

'And they even gave you a diploma?'

The man looked at Jensen in surprise.

'Yes, farcically enough. How did you know?'

'Where is it now?'

'It doesn't exist any more. I'd like to say I

tore it into tiny pieces and scattered them from the thirtieth floor but prosaically enough, I just threw it away before I left the building.'

'Did you crumple it up?'

'I wouldn't have been able to get it in the bin otherwise. It was quite a size, as I recall. Why do you ask?'

Inspector Jensen asked four further questions.

'Is this your permanent address?'

'As I told you before, I've lived here ever since the flats were built, and I'm planning to stay for as long as there's still electricity and running water. In a way it's better than before. There are no neighbours, so you don't notice how thin the walls are.'

'Why is the Special Department called Department 31?'

'Its rooms are on the thirty-first floor.'

'Is there one?'

'Yes, in the attic, between the editorial offices for the comics and the roof terrace. The lifts don't go that far.'

'Have you been there?'

'No, never. Most people don't even know it exists.'

Before they parted, the man said:

'I'm sorry I went on like that. It must have seemed naïve and muddled, the way I had to simplify and condense it all. But you would insist . . .'

And finally:

'Incidentally, am I still under suspicion for something?'

Jensen was already on the stairs and did not reply.

The man remained in the doorway. He did not seem worried, just indifferent and rather tired.

CHAPTER 19

He sat in the car for a few minutes, looking over his notes. Then he turned the page and wrote: Number 3, former chief editor, age 48, unmarried, employment terminated at own request, on full pension.

Number 3 was a woman.

The sun was shining, white and pitiless. It was Saturday, and the clock showed one minute to twelve. He had exactly thirty-six hours left. Inspector Jensen turned the key in the ignition and pulled away.

He had turned off the short-wave radio, and even though he was obliged to pass through the city centre, he did not bother to drop into the Sixteenth District station.

He did, however, stop at a snack bar, where he spent some time contemplating the three standard dishes of the day. The menus were devised in a special division of the Ministry for Public Health. The food was prepared centrally by a large food industry syndicate, and the same dishes were served at all the snack bars and restaurants. He stood in front of the electronic menu for so long that the queue grew restive behind him.

Then he pressed one of the buttons, took the loaded tray that appeared, and pushed his way through to a table.

He sat and looked at his lunch: milk, carrot juice, mince, some soggy white cabbage and two boiled potatoes cooked to a mush.

He was very hungry but dared not rely on his digestive system. After a while he put a little bit of the mince in his mouth, chewed it for a long time, drank the carrot juice, got up and went out.

The street he was heading for was in the east, not far from the centre, and in a residential part of town that had always been favoured by whatever upper class happened to exist at the time. The building was new, and not designed to the standard model. It belonged to the group, and boasted not only guest suites and conference rooms but also a large studio apartment with a terrace and skylight windows.

A dumpy little woman opened the door. Her blonde hair seemed to be fixed up in some artistic style, and her made-up face was smooth, as bright and rosy as a picture in a colour supplement. She was wearing a pink and powder blue negligee of some filmy

131

fabric. On her feet she had high-heeled red mules with gold embroidery, and peculiar, multicoloured tassels on the front.

Inspector Jensen felt he remembered precisely that outfit from a fold-out, colour picture in one of the hundred and forty-four magazines.

'Ooh, a man,' the woman giggled.

'Inspector Jensen from the Sixteenth District. I'm conducting an investigation that has to do with your former employment and place of work,' he intoned, holding up his police ID.

As he did so, he looked past the woman into the apartment.

It was a large, airy room, and the interior design looked expensive. Against a background of pastel fabrics and plants growing up a trellis were low groups of furniture made of light-coloured wood. The whole flat looked like a bedroom for the daughter of an American millionaire, abnormally enlarged and transplanted direct from an ideal home show.

On the sofa sat another woman, dark-haired and considerably younger. On one of the low tables sat a sherry bottle, a glass and an exotic species of cat.

The woman in the negligee tripped lightly into the room.

'Heavens, how exciting, a detective,' she said.

132

Jensen followed her.

'Fancy that dear, a real detective, from some special office or district or whatever it's called. Just like in one of our picture serials.'

She turned to him and chirped:

'Do sit down, dear. By all means make yourself comfy in my little lair. Now, Inspector, can I offer you a glass of sherry?'

Jensen shook his head and sat down.

'Oh, I'm forgetting that I've got company; this is one of my dear colleagues, one of those who took over the ship when I came ashore.'

The dark-haired woman gave Jensen a brief, uninterested glance. Then she turned a polite, subservient smile on the woman in the negligee. Her hostess sank on to the sofa, put her head to one side and blinked girlishly. Suddenly she said, in a cold and businesslike tone:

'How can I help?

Jensen got out his notebook and pen.

'When did you cease your employment?'

'At the end of the year. But please don't call it my employment. Being a journalist is a calling, as much as being a doctor or a priest is. One mustn't forget for a moment that the readers are our fellow human beings, almost our spiritual patients. One's life is so intensely in tune with the rhythm of our publications, and lived entirely for the readers; one had to give with one's whole heart.'

The younger woman stared at her shoes and

bit her lip. The corners of her mouth twitched, as if she were trying to suppress a scream or a smile.

'Why did you leave?'

'I left the publishing house because I felt my career was complete. I had achieved my goal, leading the magazine from triumph to triumph for twenty years. I'm not exaggerating when I say that I created it with my own hands. When I took it over it was nothing. In only a short time I had made it the biggest women's magazine in the country, and before long it was the biggest of all the magazines. And it's held on to that position.'

She looked at the dark-haired woman and said venomously:

'And how did I do it? Through work, through total self-sacrifice. One has to live for one's task, think in pictures and headlines, with every sense open to the reader's demands, to . . .'

She thought for a moment.

'To satisfy their legitimate need to gild their everyday lives with beautiful dreams, ideals and poetry.'

She took a sip of her sherry and said icily:

'To achieve that, one has to have what we call feeling. Not many people have that natural gift. Sometimes we have to harden ourselves as we look inward in order to give our all when we look outward.'

She closed her eyes. Her voice softened.

134

'All this one does with a single aim. The magazine and its readers.'

'That's two,' said Inspector Jensen.

The dark-haired woman shot him a frightened glance. Their hostess did not react.

'I presume you know how I became the editor in chief?'

'No.'

Her tone changed again, becoming almost dreamy.

'It's almost like a fairy tale. I can see it all in front of me like a real-life picture story. This is how it happened.'

Her pitch and facial expression changed again.

'My origins are simple, and I'm not ashamed of it,' she said aggressively, the corners of her mouth turned down and her nose in the air.

'I see.'

She gave her visitor a quick, appraising look and said matter-of-factly:

'The chairman of the group is a genius. Nothing less than a genius. A great man, greater than Demokratus.'

'Demokratus?'

She chirruped and waggled her head.

'Oh, me and names. I mean somebody else, of course. It's not easy when there's so much to fit in up there.'

Jensen nodded.

'The chairman took me directly from a very humble post and let me look after the

135

magazine. I mean to say, what complete madness, what boldness. Just think, a young girl like me as the head of a big editorial department. But I was the fresh new blood the magazine needed. In three months I'd knocked the department into shape, cleared out the dead wood, and within six months I'd made it every woman's favourite reading. Which it has been ever since.'

Her voice changed as she addressed herself to the woman with dark hair:

'Never forget that the eight-page horoscope, the cinemascope picture stories and the real-life series about the mothers of great men were my idea. We're still making capital out of those today. And the pets, the full-colour pull-out.'

She made a feeble gesture of self-deprecation, rings sparkling on her fingers, and said mildly:

'But I'm not saying that because I want praise or flattery. I've already got my reward, in the form of hundreds of thousands of heart-warming letters from grateful readers.'

The woman lapsed momentarily into silence, her hand raised and her head turned to one side, as if she were scanning the horizon.

'Don't ask me how you achieve something like that,' she said diffidently. 'It's something you just feel, you feel it as surely as you know that every woman at least once in her life is going to experience a look of hot, intense desire.'

The dark-haired woman gave a stifled sort of gurgle.

The woman in the negligee flinched, and stared at her with undisguised loathing.

'That was in our time, of course,' she said in a hard, patronising tone. 'When we women still had a bit of fire in our bellies.'

Her face had fallen and a network of wrinkles had emerged around her eyes and mouth. She chewed irritably on the long, pointed, shimmering silver nail of her left thumb.

'You were given a farewell diploma when you left?'

'I certainly was,' she said. 'Oh, it was just so sweet of them.' The teenage smile returned and her eyes began to twinkle.

'Would you like to see it?'

'Yes.'

She rose gracefully and floated out of the room. The dark-haired woman gave Jensen a panic-stricken look.

The woman came back with the document pressed to her chest.

'And can you imagine, every single personality of any importance signed it for me, even a real princess.'

She opened the diploma. The blank page on the left was covered in signatures.

'I think this was my very favourite, of all the

hundreds of presents I got. From all over, do you want to see?'

'There's no need,' said Jensen.

The woman smiled, bashful and bewildered.

'But why have you, a police inspector, come here to ask me all this?'

'I'm not at liberty to discuss that,' said Inspector Jensen.

Her face went through a whole series of fleeting expressions. Finally she threw out her hands in a gesture of helpless femininity, and said submissively:

'Well I suppose I must resign myself.'

He was accompanied back down by the woman with dark hair. No sooner was the lift in motion than the girl gave a sob and said:

'Don't believe a word she says. She's horrible, ghastly, a monster. There are the most disgusting stories going round about her.'

'I see.'

'She's a monstrosity, so spiteful, so nosy. She's still pulling all the strings, even since they managed to get her out of the building. Now she's forcing me to be her spy. Every Wednesday and Saturday I have to come here and give her a complete report. She wants to know it all.'

'Why are you doing it?'

'Why? Good God, she could wipe me out in under ten minutes, the way you squash a louse. She wouldn't hesitate for an instant. And all the while she insults me. Oh God.'

138

Inspector Jensen said nothing. When they reached the ground floor, he doffed his hat and opened the doors. The young woman gave him a shy look and scuttled out into the street.

There was noticeably less traffic. It was Saturday. The time was five minutes to four. The right side of his diaphragm was hurting.

CHAPTER 20

Inspector Jensen had switched off the engine, but was still sitting in the car, his notebook open on the steering wheel in front of him. He had just written: Number 4, art director, unmarried, age 20, employment terminated at own request.

Number 4 was also a woman.

The building was on the other side of the street. It was not brand new, but had been well maintained. He found the right door, conveniently located on the ground floor, and rang the bell. No one answered. He rang a couple more times, then knocked long and hard. Finally he tried the handle. The door was locked. Not a sound had come from inside. He stood there for a minute or two. While he was waiting, a telephone started to ring inside the flat. He returned to the car, left five pages of his pad blank and then wrote: Number 5, age 52, journalist, unmarried, left at the end of the agreed contract period.

This time he was lucky with the address: the street was in the same part of town and he only had to drive five blocks.

The building was just like the one he had been in ten minutes previously, long and yellow, five storeys high and set at an angle to the road. The whole district consisted of similar blocks of flats with laminated wood exteriors.

The sign on the door panel was made of letters cut from a newspaper or magazine and fixed on with sticky tape. Some of them had disintegrated or fallen off, making the name illegible. The bell worked, but although he could hear someone moving about inside the flat, it was several minutes before the door was opened.

The man looked older than expected. What was more, he looked extremely unkempt, with matted hair in need of a cut, and a shaggy grey beard. He was wearing a grubby, off-white shirt, drooping trousers and worn black shoes. Inspector Jensen frowned. It was very unusual nowadays for people to be poorly dressed.

'Inspector Jensen from the Sixteenth District. I'm conducting an investigation that has to do with your former employment and place of work.'

He did not bother to get out his ID.

'Can you show me your ID?' the man said at once.

140

Jensen showed him the enamel tag.

'Come in,' said the man.

He seemed self-confident, almost arrogant.

The mess in the flat was remarkable. The floors were covered in loose sheets of paper, newspapers, books, old oranges, bulging rubbish sacks, dirty clothes and unwashed cups, plates and dishes. The furniture comprised a couple of upright wooden chairs, two sagging armchairs, a rickety table and a sofa with an untidy jumble of bedclothes on it. One half of the table had been cleared, obviously to make space for a typewriter and a pile of typescript. There was a layer of thick, greyish dust over everything. The atmosphere was stuffy. And it smelt of alcohol. The man cleared the other half of the table with the aid of a folded newspaper. The indeterminable pile of paper, household articles and other junk fell to the floor.

'Sit here,' he said, pushing forward a chair.

'You are inebriated,' said Inspector Jensen.

'Not drunk. Under the influence of alcohol. I never get drunk, but I'm under the influence most of the time. There's quite a difference.'

Inspector Jensen sat down. The bearded man stood diagonally behind him.

'You're a good observer, or you wouldn't have noticed,' he said. 'Most people don't.'

'When did you leave your employment?'

'Two months ago. Why do you ask?'

Jensen put his spiral-bound pad on the table

141

and leafed through it. As he reached the page with Number 3, the man came up behind his back.

'I'm in select company, I see.'

Jensen continued turning the pages.

'It amazes me you got away from that cow with your reason intact,' said the man, walking round the table. 'Did you go to her place? I'd never dare.'

'You know her?'

'Are you joking? I was working on that magazine when she arrived. When she was made chief editor. And I survived for nearly a whole year.'

'Survived?'

'I was younger and stronger then, of course.'

He sat down on the sofa bed, thrust his right arm into the tangle of dirty bed linen and pulled out the bottle.

'Since you've noticed anyway, it doesn't make any difference. And anyway, as I told you, I'm not drunk. Just a bit more on the ball.'

Jensen had his eyes fixed on him.

The man took a few swigs from the bottle, set it down and said:

'What are you after?'

'Some information.'

'What about?'

Jensen didn't answer.

'If it's that bitch you want to know about, you've come to the right address. Not many people know her better than me. I could write her biography.'

The man stopped, but did not seem to be expecting an answer. He peered at his visitor through screwed-up eyes, then at the window, which was almost opaque with filth. Despite the alcohol, his look was observant and alert.

'Do you know how it happened, when she was put in charge of the biggest magazine in the country?'

Jensen said nothing.

'Shame,' said the man. 'Nothing like enough people do. And yet it's one of the major turning points in the history of the press.'

The room went quiet for a moment. Jensen regarded the man indifferently and twirled his plastic biro between his fingers.

'Do you know what her job was before she became chief editor?'

He gave a spiteful laugh.

'Cleaning lady. And do you know where she cleaned?'

Jensen drew a very small, five-pointed star on the empty page of his notepad.

'In the holiest of holies. The management suite. How she'd managed to get put there, of all places, I don't know, but I'm sure it was no coincidence.'

He leaned down and picked up the bottle.

'She could arrange most things. You know, she was attractive, damn attractive so everyone thought until they'd known her for five minutes.'

He drank.

'In those days, the cleaning was always done after office hours. The cleaners came at six. All of them except her. She got there an hour early, when the chairman was generally still in his office. He liked to send the secretaries home on the dot of five and then spend some time on something he didn't want anyone else to see. I don't know what.

'But I've got a pretty good idea,' he said, looking towards the window.

The room had darkened. Jensen looked at his watch. It was a quarter past six.

'At exactly a quarter past five she'd open the door to the chairman's office, look in and say sorry, then shut it again. Whenever he was on his way out, or going to the toilet or something, he'd always see her disappear round a corner of the corridor.'

Inspector Jensen opened his mouth to say something, but instantly thought the better of it.

'She was particularly attractive from behind, you see. I remember vividly what she used to look like. She had a pale blue cleaning overall and white clogs and a white headscarf, and she was always bare-legged. Presumably she'd heard the talk. I remember it was said that the chairman couldn't resist the sight of the back of a pair of knees.'

The man got up, took a couple of sticky steps and switched on the light.

'That hadn't been going on very long before the chairman started making passes at her; he was known to be quite vigorous in that department. They say he always introduces himself first, absurdly enough. But do you know what happened?'

The light bulb hanging from the ceiling was coated in a greasy layer of dust and shed a faint, roving light.

'She never answered when he spoke to her, just mumbled something shy and incomprehensible and gave him that doe-eyed look. She carried on exactly as before.'

Jensen drew another star. With six points.

'He became obsessed with her. He did everything he possibly could. Tried to find out her address. He couldn't. God knows where she hid away. They say he sent people to shadow her, but she outwitted them. Then she started coming a quarter of an hour later. He was still there. She came later and later, and he would generally be sitting in his room, pretending to be busy with something. So finally . . .'

He paused. Jensen waited thirty seconds. Then he raised his eyes and looked expressionlessly at the man on the sofa bed.

'He was going out of his mind, see. One evening it was half past eight before she came, and by then all the other cleaners had finished and gone home. The light in his room was off, but she knew he was there because she'd seen his outdoor things. So she clumped up and down the corridor in her clogs a few times, and then she picked up her bloody bucket and went in and closed the door behind her.'

He laughed to himself, a low chuckle.

'It's too bloody good to be true,' he said. 'The chairman was standing behind the door in his string vest, and he threw himself at her with a bellow and tore off her clothes and sent her bucket flying and threw her to the ground and screwed her. She struggled and yelled and . . .'

The man broke off and regarded his visitor triumphantly.

'And what do you think happened?'

Jensen was looking at something on the floor. It was impossible to tell whether he was listening.

'Well just then, in comes a uniformed night-time security guard with a bunch of keys on his belt and shines his torch. When he sees who it is, he's scared to death and slams the door and runs off, and the chairman runs after him. The guard dives into a lift and the chairman just manages to get in there with him as the doors close. He thinks the guard's going to sound the alarm but the poor wretch is terrified and thinks he's going to lose his job. She'd planned it all in advance, of course, and knew to the second when he came on his rounds and clocked in on that floor.'

The man gave a gurgle of suppressed laughter and squirmed among the tangled bedclothes.

'Just imagine the chairman standing in the lift in nothing but a string vest with a petrified security guard in a uniform and peaked cap, with a torch and a truncheon and a big bunch of keys on his belt. They go all the way down to the paper store before either of them has the presence of mind to press the stop button and get the lift to go back up again. And when they get back, the guard isn't a guard any more but the security manager of the whole site, even though he didn't dare utter a word the whole way.'

The storyteller fell silent. The sparkle in his eyes seemed to fade. He said resignedly:

'The old security manager got the sack for hiring deficient staff.

'Well, then came the negotiations of terms and conditions, and she must have played her cards brilliantly, because a week later an internal memo comes round, saying our chief editor's been replaced, and a quarter of an hour later she sweeps into the editorial office and all hell breaks loose.'

The man appeared to remember the bottle, and took a cautious little swig.

'You see, the magazine was really pretty good, but it wasn't selling well. Even though it was all about princesses and how to make ginger snaps, it went over the readers' heads, was how they put it, and there had been talk of closing it down. But . . .'

He gave his visitor a searching look, as if

trying to make contact, but Jensen did not meet his eye.

'It was pure *Kristallnacht*, what she did then. Practically the entire staff was weeded out and replaced by a pack of complete idiots. We had a sub-editor who was really a hairdresser and had never seen a semicolon. When she happened to see one on her typewriter, she came into my office and asked me what it was and I was so scared of getting the sack I didn't dare tell her. I recall I told her it was just another example of intellectual snobbery.'

He ground his toothless jaws for a while.

'The old cow hated anything intellectual, see, and according to her, almost everything was intellectual, and especially being able to write coherent sentences on a piece of paper. The only reason I survived was that I didn't seem like the others. Plus the fact that I minded every single word I said. There was a newly hired reporter who was stupid enough to pass on some story about one of the other bosses, to ingratiate himself. It was something that had really happened, mind you, and it was a bloody funny story. A man from the ideas department had come up to the editorial office of the arts pages of one of the biggest papers and said August Strindberg was a hell of a good writer and his film *Miss Julie* would make a great picture serial if they rewrote it a bit and got rid of all the class barriers and other incomprehensible stuff. The arts editor thought for a minute and then he said, "What did you say the writer was called?" And the ideas guy said: "August Strindberg, you know." And then the arts editor said, "Oh yeah, him. Well, tell him to come to the Grand tomorrow at twelve and we'll have lunch and talk about the price." So that reporter passed the story on, and she just gave him an icy cool look and said, "What's so funny about that, then?" And two hours later he had to clear his desk and go.'

The man started chuckling to himself again. Inspector Jensen raised his eyes and regarded him expressionlessly.

'But then we get to the clever bit. With her matchless stupidity, she managed to double the circulation within a year. The magazine filled up with pictures of dogs and children and cats and pot plants; with horoscopes and phrenology and how to read fortunes in coffee grounds and water geraniums, and there wasn't a comma in the right place, but people bought it. You see, what little there was that could be called text was so incredibly over-explicit and naïve that it'd be a match for anything being written today. You couldn't write the bloody word locomotive without explaining it was a machine on wheels that ran on metal tracks and pulled carriages. And it proved a major, decisive victory for the chairman. Everyone said his boldness and foresight were extraordinary, and that his move had revolutionised journalism training through and through, and changed the very principles of modern newspaper and magazine publishing.'

He took another swig from the bottle.

'It was perfect. The only fly in the ointment was the night guard. He was tremendously proud of his new post and couldn't keep quiet about how he'd got it. But he didn't get to go on about it for long. Six months later he was crushed to death in the paternoster lift. It stopped between two floors, and as he was crawling out, it started again. He was more or less chopped in half. And colossally stupid as he was, there can be no doubting it was his own fault.'

The man put his hand in front of his mouth and had a long, hacking fit of coughing. When the attack was over, he said:

'And then she went on being bloody-minded, year after year. Her tastes got more and more refined, would you believe it, and her pretensions went on growing, and the magazine was stuffed fuller and fuller of pictures of unwearable clothes. The fashion companies bribed her, everyone said. In the end they managed to get rid of her, but it wasn't cheap. They say the chairman had to stump up a quarter of a million in ready money to get her to agree to early retirement on a pension to match her salary.'

'Why did you leave?' said Inspector Jensen.

'What does it matter?'

'Why did you leave?'

The bottle was empty. The man shook himself and said with feeling:

'I got the sack. Just like that. Without any compensation, after all those years.'

'For what reason?'

'They wanted to get rid of me. I suppose I looked too scruffy for them. I wasn't a worthy ambassador for the company. And anyway, I'm burnt out as a writer, haven't another line in me, not even drivel. It happens to everyone.'

'Was that the immediate reason?'

'No.'

'What was the immediate reason you were sacked?'

'I was drinking in my office.'

'And you had to leave straight away?'

'Yes. Formally I wasn't dismissed, of course. My contract was drawn up in a way that meant they could send me packing whenever they wanted to.'

'And you didn't protest?'

'No.'

'Why?'

'There was no point. They've got themselves a new head of personnel, who used to be the leader of the journalists' union and still directs it. He knows all the loopholes; no mere mortal stands a chance. If you're going to appeal, you have to do it indirectly, to him, and he's the

151

one who decides. It's smart, but it's the same with everything. Their tax lawyers also hold positions at the Ministry of Finance, and the criticism of the weekly magazines that does crop up every five years is actually written by them, in their own newspapers. But that's how it is with everything.'

'Did it make you feel bitter?'

'I don't think so. The time for that's passed. Who feels bitter these days?'

'You got some kind of farewell diploma when you left?'

'I may have. They like to do things in style. The head of personnel's an expert at stuff like that. He smiles, and offers you a cigar with one hand while throttling you with the other. And he looks like a toad, by the way.'

The man was losing his focus.

'You got a diploma, didn't you?'

'I think so.'

'Have you still got it?'

'I don't know.'

'Show it to me.'

'I won't, and I can't.'

'Is it here in the flat?'

'I don't know. And even if it was, I wouldn't be able to find it. Would you be able to find anything in here?'

Inspector Jensen looked about him. Then he shut his notebook and got to his feet.

'Goodbye,' he said.

'You still haven't told me why you came

here.'

Jensen did not answer. He took his hat and left the room. The man just sat there among the dirty bedclothes. He looked grey and worn, and his eyes were dim.

Inspector Jensen turned on the car radio, called for an emergency vehicle and gave the address.

'Yes,' he said. 'Domestic alcohol abuse. Take him to the main station in the Sixteenth District. And be quick about it.'

On the other side of the street there was a telephone kiosk. He went over to it and rang the head of the plainclothes patrol.

'I want the flat searched. And be quick about it. You know what you're looking for.'

'Yes, Inspector.'

'Then get back to the station and wait. Detain him until you receive further orders.'

'On what grounds?'

'Anything you like.'

'Understood.'

Inspector Jensen returned to his car. He had gone no more than fifty metres when he met the police van.

CHAPTER 21

Light was seeping out through the letterbox. Inspector Jensen took out his notebook and

153

reread what he had written: Number 4, art director, unmarried, age 20, employment terminated at own request. Then he put the pad away, got out his police ID and rang the doorbell.

'Who is it?'

'Police.'

'Rubbish. I keep saying there's no point asking. I don't want to.'

'Open up.'

'Never, I don't want to!'

'Open up.'

'Go away. Leave me in peace, for God's sake. Tell him I don't want to!'

Jensen administered two heavy blows to the door.

'Police. Open up.'

The door swung open and she gave him a sceptical stare.

'No,' she said. 'Things have gone too damn far this time.'

He took a step over the threshold and showed his ID.

'Inspector Jensen from the Sixteenth District,' he said. 'I'm conducting an investigation that has to do with your former employment and place of work.'

She stared at his enamel badge and backed into the flat.

She was a young woman, with dark hair, shallow-set grey eyes and a firm jawline. She was wearing a checked shirt, khaki trousers

154

and a pair of boots. She was long-legged and strikingly slim-waisted, but her hips looked broad. As she moved, it was evident she had nothing else on under the shirt. Her hair was short and tousled, and she clearly did not use make-up.

She somehow reminded him of women in pictures from the old days.

The expression in her eyes was hard to read. It seemed to contain anger, fear, desperation and decision in equal measure.

Her trousers were smeared with paint, and she had a brush in her hand. There was newspaper spread in the centre of the floor, and on it stood a rocking chair that she was evidently in the process of painting.

Jensen looked about him. The rest of the furniture, too, looked as though it had been found on the rubbish dump by someone who had then painted it in cheerful colours.

'So you weren't lying,' she said. 'He's even set the police on me, now. I might have known it. But I want to make one thing plain from the start. You can't scare me. Lock me up if you can find an excuse. I've got a bottle of wine in the kitchen, maybe that'll do. It makes no odds. Anything's better than going on like this.'

Inspector Jensen got out his notebook.

'When did you cease your employment?' he asked.

'A fortnight ago. I just stopped bothering to

turn up. Is there a law against that?'

'How long had you been employed by the group?'

'Two weeks. Have you got any other stupid questions to plague me with? I've told you, you won't get anywhere.'

'Why did you leave?'

'Good grief, what do you think? Because I couldn't stand being nagged every minute of the day and chased with every step I took.'

'You were an art director?'

'I most certainly wasn't; I was an assistant in a layout department, what they call a glue girl. I didn't even have time to learn that job properly before this business blew up.'

'What does being an art director involve?'

'I don't know. I think you copy lettering and whole pages out of foreign papers.'

'Exactly why did you leave your job?'

'Good grief, are they giving the police orders now? Can't you show a bit of pity? Tell your employer there are clinics that would certainly be better places for him than my bed.'

'Why did you leave?'

'I left because I couldn't stand it any longer. Can't you try to understand? He had his eye on me from a couple of days after I started. A photographer I knew had asked me to be the model for a picture to go with some kind of medical investigation or something. And he'd seen the picture. He took me in his car to a funny little restaurant in the middle of

156

nowhere. Then I let him come here, stupidly enough. The next night he rang—*he* rang *me*, I mean—and asked me if I'd got a bottle of wine in the house. I told him to go to hell, of course. And so it went on.'

She stood in the middle of the floor, feet planted wide apart, and stared at him.

'What in Christ's name do you want to know? That he sat over there on the floor babbling away for three hours, holding my foot? And that he almost had a heart attack when I struggled free and went off to bed?'

'You are supplying a lot of superfluous information.'

She tossed the paintbrush down beside the chair, and a few red splashes landed on her boots.

'Yes, well,' she said nervously. 'I suppose I would have slept with him when it came to it. Why not? A person has to have some interests in life. I was sleepy, of course, but how was I to know he'd go to pieces like that, just because I took my clothes off. Don't you realise what hell it's been for me these last few weeks, day after day? He's got to have me. He's got to have my simple, natural urges. He'll send me round the world. I've got to help him find something he's lost. He'll put me in charge of God knows what. In charge, me! No darling, you don't have to be able to do anything. Not interested? It doesn't matter, darling.'

'I repeat: you are supplying a lot of
157

superfluous information.'

She finally held her breath and looked at him with a puzzled frown.

'You haven't come . . . it wasn't him who sent you?'

'No. You were given some kind of farewell diploma when you left?'

'Yes, but . . .'

'Show it to me.'

She looked entirely baffled. She went over to a blue chest of drawers against one wall, opened a drawer and took out the certificate.

'It's a bit of a mess,' she said tentatively.

Jensen opened it. Someone had dotted the gold text with big red exclamation marks. On the last page a few obscene slogans had been scrawled in red pen.

'I know it's not the done thing, but I was livid. It was all so ridiculous. I'd only been there a fortnight, and all I'd done was let my foot be held for three hours and get undressed and put my pyjamas on.'

Inspector Jensen put his notebook back in his pocket.

'Goodbye,' he said.

As he was going out of the front door into the hallway he felt the pain on the right-hand side of his diaphragm. It was sudden and searing. His vision went; he took a tentative step and had to lean his shoulder on the doorpost.

She was there at once.

'What is it?' she said. 'Are you ill? Come and sit down a minute. Here, let me help you.'

He stood where he was, aware of her body. She was close beside him, supporting him. He noted that she was soft and warm.

'Wait,' she said. 'I'll get some water.'

She hurried out into the kitchen and came straight back.

'Here, drink some of this. Is there anything I can do? Would you like to rest for a while? I'm sorry I behaved like that, but you see, I misunderstood completely. One of that lot at the top who make all the decisions, I won't say which, has been after me the whole time.'

Jensen straightened up. The pain was as bad as ever, but he had started to get used to it.

'I apologise,' she said. 'But I didn't understand what you wanted. I still don't, in fact. Blast, everything always turns out wrong. I get so worried sometimes that there's something wrong with me, that I'm not like other people. But I want an interest, want to do something of my own, and decide for myself what it's going to be. I was different at school, and nobody understood when I asked about things. I was just interested. I'm different, not like other women, I'm always noticing it. It's true, and I look different as well, I even smell different. Either I'm crazy or the world is, and either way it's bad.'

The pain slowly eased.

'You should mind your tongue,' said

159

Inspector Jensen.

He took his hat and went out to the car.

CHAPTER 22

While Inspector Jensen was driving back into the city, he contacted the duty officer in the Sixteenth District. The officers sent to search the flat had still not come back. The chief of police had tried to contact him several times during the day.

When he got back to the city centre it was already past eleven, the traffic was thinning out and there were only a few pedestrians on the pavements. The pain in his diaphragm had receded and was now the usual dull, persistent ache. His mouth felt dry, and as always after an attack he was extremely thirsty. He stopped at one of the snack bars that were still open, sat at the glass counter and ordered a bottle of mineral water. The place was gleaming, with mirrored walls. It was empty apart from half a dozen young people in their late teens. They were sitting round a table, staring apathetically and saying nothing. The man serving behind the counter was yawning and reading one of the one hundred and forty-four magazines, a comic. Three TV sets were showing a harmless light entertainment programme with the mechanical blare of canned laughter.

He drank the mineral water slowly, in small gulps, and felt the liquid generate griping sensations and bubbling chain reactions in his empty stomach. After a while he got up and went to the toilet. By the urinal a well-dressed man was lying on his back with one arm in the drainage channel. He stank of alcohol and had thrown up on his jacket and shirt. His eyes were open but his gaze was fixed and unseeing.

Jensen returned to the counter.

'There's an inebriated man in the urinal,' he said.

The man behind the bar shrugged and continued to scan the row of brightly coloured TV screens.

Jensen showed his ID. The man immediately put down his comic and went over to the police telephone. All the food outlets had a direct line to the officer on radio duty at the nearest station.

The constables who came to fetch the drunk looked worn out from lack of sleep. When they carried the man out to arrest him, his head banged several times on the imitation marble floor. They were from a different police district, probably the eleventh, and did not recognise Inspector Jensen.

The clock showed five to twelve as the barman turned a timid look on his customers and began to close for the night. Jensen went out to the car and called the duty office in the Sixteenth District. The patrol had just returned from searching the flat.

'Yes,' said the head of the plainclothes patrol, 'we found it.'

'Intact?'

'Yes, or at any rate, all the pages were there. There was a trampled frankfurter squashed between them, of course.'

Jensen sat in silence for a moment.

'It took a long time,' said the head of the plainclothes patrol, 'but then, it wasn't an easy job. What a dump. Millions of bits of paper.'

'Make sure the owner of the flat is released in the normal way first thing tomorrow.'

'Understood.'

'One other thing.'

'Yes, Inspector.'

'Some years ago, the site security manager died in one of the lifts.'

'Yes.'

'Look into the circumstances. And find out what you can about the man, particularly his family situation. Be quick about it.'

'Understood. Inspector?'

'Yes.'

'I think the police chief's been trying to get hold of you.'

'Did he leave a message?'

'Not as far as I know.'

'Goodnight.'

He hung up. Somewhere nearby, a clock struck twelve, a harsh, piercing peal.

The sixth day was over. He had exactly twenty-four hours left.

CHAPTER 23

Inspector Jensen took it easy on the way home. He was physically tired, but knew he was going to find it very hard to sleep. Moreover, he only had a few hours left.

He did not meet a single vehicle in the long road tunnel, which was whitewashed and brightly lit, and further south the huge industrial area stood silent and deserted. The aluminium tanks and the Plexiglas roofs of the factories glinted in the moonlight.

On the bridge he was overtaken by a police van, with an ambulance right behind it. They were both driving fast, sirens whining.

Halfway along the motorway he had to stop at a police roadblock. The constable with the stop light clearly recognised him; when Jensen wound down the side window, the man stood to attention and said:

'Traffic accident. One dead. The crash vehicle's blocking the carriageway. We'll have it clear in a few minutes.'

Jensen nodded. He sat with the window open, letting the raw night air stream into the car. While he waited, he thought about the accidents, declining in number from year to year while the number of fatalities continued to rise. The experts at the Ministry of Communications had long since solved this statistical conundrum. The decrease in collisions and material damage could to some extent be accounted for by better roads and enhanced traffic surveillance. More important was the psychological factor: people had become more and more reliant on their cars, treating them with greater care and reacting almost subconsciously to the thought of losing them. The rising number of deaths was explained by the fact that most fatal crashes were really to be classified as suicide. Here, too, the psychological factor played a decisive role: people lived with and for their cars, and also wanted to die with them. This had been the finding of a study carried out some years before. It was marked top secret, but senior police officers had been given access to the information.

Eight minutes later, the carriageway was clear; he wound up the window and drove on. The road surface was covered with a fine layer of hoar frost, and at the crash site the tyre tracks were clearly visible in the arc lights. They showed no evidence of skidding or braking, but ran straight into a concrete column at the side of the road. The insurance would in all likelihood never be paid out. And yet, as always, the possibility remained that the driver had been tired and had fallen asleep at the wheel.

Inspector Jensen felt vaguely dissatisfied, as if there were something missing. When he tried to analyse the phenomenon, he became aware of a hollow feeling of hunger. He parked the car outside the seventh tower block in the third row, went to the snack vending machine and pressed the button for a packet of a powdered nutrition drink for dieters.

Up in the flat he hung up his outdoor clothes and jacket and switched on the light. Then he pulled down the window blinds, went into the kitchen, measured thirty centilitres of water into a pan and whisked in the powder. When the drink was hot, he poured it into a teacup and went back to the main room, put the cup on his bedside table, sat on the bed and unlaced his shoes. The clock showed a quarter past two, and the whole block of flats was silent. He still had a sense that something was missing.

He fetched his spiral-bound notebook from his jacket pocket, switched on the reading lamp above his bed and turned off the overhead light. Sipping the nutrition drink, he read slowly and systematically through his notes. The drink was thick and sticky and had a stale, insipid taste.

Once he had finished reading, he raised his eyes and looked at one of the framed photographs from the police training college. He was in the picture, second from the right in the back row. He was standing with his arms folded, smiling a fuzzy smile. He must have been saying something to the person next to him just as the photographer took the picture.

A little while later, he stood up and went out into the hall. He opened the wardrobe door and took one of the bottles that were lined up along the back, behind the police caps on the hat shelf. Then he went to get a glass from the kitchen, filled it almost to the brim with spirits and put it beside the cup of instant gruel.

He unfolded the list of the nine names and put it in front of him on the table. He sat motionless, studying it.

The electric clock on the wall marked the time with three short rings.

Inspector Jensen turned to a new page of the notebook and wrote: Number 6, age 38, divorced, PR man, transferred to other activities.

As he noted down the address, he gave an almost imperceptible shake of the head.

Then he set the alarm clock, put out the light and undressed. He pulled on his pyjamas and sat on the bed with the blanket over his legs. The gruel seemed to swell up in his stomach and he felt as if something was pressing upwards against his heart.

He picked up his tumbler and drained it in two draughts. The spirit, sixty-three per cent proof, burnt into his tongue and sank down his throat like a pillar of fire.

He lay on his back in the dark, eyes wide open, waiting for rest.

CHAPTER 24

Inspector Jensen did not fall asleep. From three o'clock to twenty past five he lay in a sort of stupor, unable to think clearly and yet incapable of disconnecting his thought processes. When the alarm clock rang, he felt queasy and found he was drenched in sweat. Forty minutes later, he was sitting in the car.

The place he had to get to lay two hundred kilometres to the north, and since it was Sunday he reckoned he ought to be there in three hours.

The city was silent and desolate, its multi-storey car parks empty and its parking spaces naked, but the traffic lights worked away as usual and as he drove through the centre he found himself stopping for ten red lights.

The motorway was straight, the driving trouble-free, and the scenery on either side uninteresting. Here and there he saw distant suburbs or self-clearance estates silhouetted against the sky. From the horizon to the motorway, the ground was covered in an expanse of dry and dreary vegetation: deformed trees and low, scrubby bushes.

At eight o'clock, Inspector Jensen turned into a service station to fill up with petrol. He also drank a cup of lukewarm tea and made two phone calls.

The head of the plainclothes patrol sounded tired and hoarse, and had clearly been roused from his sleep.

'It was nineteen years ago,' he said. 'The man got stuck in a lift and was crushed to death.'

'Have we still got the file on the case?'

'Only a routine investigation noted in the log. It was evidently an open and shut case. A pure accident seemed the likeliest explanation, a chance cut in the power supply which made the lift stop for a couple of minutes and then start again of its own accord. And anyway, the man seems to have been entirely useless.'

'And his surviving relatives?'

'He had no family. Lived in a bachelors' hostel.'

'Did he leave anything?'

'Yes. A pretty large sum of money, actually.'

'Who inherited?'

'No relatives came forward within the prescribed time. In the end the money went to some state fund or other.'

'Anything else?'

'Nothing that seems significant. The fellow was a recluse, lived alone, had no friends.'

'Goodbye.'

The man who had been sent to go through the newspaper archives was also at home.

'Jensen here.'

'Yes, Inspector.'

'Any results?'

'Didn't you get my report, sir?'

'No.'

'I handed it in yesterday afternoon.'

'Give me a verbal report now.'

'Yes of course,' said the man. 'Just a minute while I try to remember.'

'Yes.'

'The cut-out letters that were used all come from the same paper, but not all from the same day. They were taken from two different issues, the Friday and the Saturday papers of last week. The typeface is called Bodoni.'

Jensen got out his spiral-bound notebook and wrote the information on the inside cover.

'Anything else?'

The man was quiet for a moment. Then he said:

'Yes, one more thing. The required combination of letters and text on the back page wasn't in all the editions of the paper. It was only in the so-called A edition.'

'Which implies what?'

'It means that the letters were only in the copies of the paper that were printed last. The ones that are sent out to vendors and subscribers here in the city.'

'You're released from the investigation,'

said Inspector Jensen. 'Return to normal duties. Goodbye.'

He hung up, went out to the car and drove on.

At nine he passed through a densely built up area, quiet at this early hour on a Sunday, but consisting of perhaps a thousand identical terraced houses, grouped in a rectangle round a factory. From the factory chimneys rose fluffy columns of yellowish smoke. A hundred or so metres in the air, the vapour cloud flattened out and sank back down over the community.

A quarter of an hour later he was at his destination.

So his calculation of the journey time had proved correct. The stop at the petrol station must have taken about fifteen minutes.

The house was a modern weekend cottage, with large picture windows and a roof of corrugated plastic. It lay on a hillside three kilometres east of the motorway, surrounded by trees. At the bottom of the hill there were glimpses of a lake of dirty brown water. The air was fouled by the stench of the factory.

On the concrete area in front of the house stood a plumpish man in his dressing gown and slippers. He seemed sluggish and lethargic, and regarded his visitor without enthusiasm. Inspector Jensen showed his ID.

'Inspector Jensen from the Sixteenth District. I'm conducting an investigation that

170

has to do with your former employment and place of work.'

'What do you want?'

'A few questions.'

'All right, come in,' he said.

The two rooms contained a number of rugs, ashtrays and items of steel furniture that looked as if they had been transported there from the publishing house.

Jensen took out his notebook and pen.

'When did you cease your employment?'

The other man stifled a yawn and looked about him, as if trying to avoid something.

'Three months ago,' he said finally.

'Why did you leave?'

The man regarded Jensen. There was a musing look in his shallow-set grey eyes. He seemed to be weighing up whether to answer or not. At length he waved a vague hand and said:

'If it's the diploma you want to see, I haven't got it here.'

Jensen said nothing.

'I left it in my wife's flat in town.'

'Why did you leave?'

The man furrowed his brow as if trying to concentrate. Eventually he said:

'Listen, whatever you've heard and whatever you're imagining, it's wrong. I can't help you with anything.'

A few seconds passed in silence. The man rubbed the tip of his nose unhappily.

171

'I haven't really left. My contract with the company has expired, admittedly, but I'm still linked to the group.'

'What work are you doing?'

Jensen looked around the bare room. The other man followed his gaze. After another silence, longer than the first, the man said:

'Listen, what's the point of all this? I don't know anything that could be of any use to you. I swear the diploma's still in town.'

'Why would I want to see your diploma?'

'Don't ask me. It seems very odd that you'd drive two hundred kilometres for a thing like that.'

The man shook his head.

'How long did it take you, by the way?'

He said it with a hint of interest, but Jensen did not reply and the man reverted to his earlier tone.

'My best time's an hour and fifty-eight minutes,' he said gloomily.

'Have you got a telephone here?'

'No, there isn't one.'

'Do you own this house?'

'No.'

'Who owns it?'

'The group. I've been lent it. I'm supposed to be having a good rest before I take on my new duties.'

'What duties?'

The answers had been getting increasingly hesitant. Now they seemed to have stopped altogether.

'Do you like it here?'

The man cast Jensen a plaintive look.

'Listen, I told you, didn't I, that you've got completely the wrong end of the stick. All those stories are groundless, believe me.'

'Which stories?'

'Well, whatever it is you've heard.'

Jensen kept his eyes fixed on the man. There wasn't a sound in the room. The smell of the factory was as pungent inside the house as it had been on the terrace.

'What post did you hold within the group?'

'Oh, a bit of everything. Sports reporter first. Then I was editor in chief of a few papers. Then I got into the advertising side. Travelled a lot, mostly sports features from all over the world. Then I was at various branch offices abroad, and then ... well, I went on study trips.'

'What did you study?'

'A bit of everything. Public relations and that kind of thing.'

'What does it involve, public relations?'

'That's not very easy to explain.'

'So you've travelled a lot?'

'I've been almost everywhere.'

'Do you speak many foreign languages?'

'No, I'm not much good at languages.'

Inspector Jensen sat for a moment, saying nothing. He did not take his eyes off the man in the dressing gown. Finally he said:

'Do the magazines and papers publish many

173

sports features?'

'No.'

The man was looking more and more miserable.

'Nobody's interested in sport these days, except on TV.'

'And yet you travelled all over the world writing sports features?'

'I've never been able to write anything else. I tried, but I couldn't.'

'Why did you stop?'

'It got too expensive, I think.'

The man thought for a few seconds.

'They're pretty mean, when all's said and done,' he said, mournfully contemplating the furniture.

'What postal district are we in here?'

The man looked at Jensen, nonplussed. Then he gestured towards the window. Above the woods on the other side of the lake hung the cloud of yellow smoke from the factory.

'The same as over there. The postman comes from there, at any rate.'

'Is there a collection every day?'

'Not on Sundays.'

The only sounds to be heard were the man's breathing and the distant roar of the cars on the motorway.

'Do you have to carry on tormenting me like this? It serves no purpose.'

'Do you know why I've come here?'

'No idea.'

The man in the dressing gown shifted uneasily. The silence seemed to trouble him.

'I'm just a plain, ordinary bloke who ran into bad luck,' he said.

'Bad luck?'

'Yes, bad luck. Everyone says the opposite, thinks I got lucky. But you can see for yourself, sitting here mouldering away all on my own, what sort of good luck is that?'

'What do you want to do?'

'Nothing. I don't want to be a bother to anyone.'

The silence grew long and oppressive. A couple of times the man in the dressing gown gave Jensen a faintly desperate look, but each time he immediately looked away.

'Please go now,' he said in an undertone. 'I swear the diploma's in town. In my wife's flat.'

'You don't seem happy here.'

'I didn't say that.'

'Were you unhappy at work?'

'No, no, not at all. Why should I have been? I mean to say, I got whatever I wanted.'

He seemed to drift off into vague brooding. Eventually he said:

'You're misunderstanding everything. You've heard those stories and you think something, I don't know what. And anyhow, it's not at all like people say. It simply isn't true. Not all of it, at any rate.'

'So the claims that are made about you aren't true?'

'Okay, if you bloody well insist, the boss did get petrified and jump overboard. But that was hardly my fault, was it?'

'When did this happen?'

'During the regatta, you know that as well as I do. It wasn't anything particularly remarkable. He took me along because he thought I knew how to sail. I suppose he wanted to win. And when we had that sudden squall and I got up on to the rail to hang out, I suppose he thought we were going to capsize, and he gave a howl and jumped in the sea. And as for me, all I could do was carry on.'

He gave Jensen a gloomy look.

'If I'd only been able to keep quiet about it, nothing would've happened. But I thought it was a funny story. And then I was so fed up when I realised I only got the plum jobs because they wanted to keep me well out of the way. And I couldn't keep quiet about that, either, but what . . .'

He gave a start, and rubbed his nose.

'Take no notice of those stories. It's all just talk. My wife cashed in on it, but then she does as she likes, doesn't she? We're divorced now, anyway. I'm not complaining. Don't think that, whatever you do.'

After a short pause he said:

'No, I'm not.'

'Show me the telegram.'

The man in the dressing gown gave Jensen a frightened stare.

'What telegram? I haven't . . .'

'Don't lie.'

The man stood up violently and went over to the window. He clenched his fists and beat them against each other.

'No,' he said. 'No, you're not going to trick me. I'm saying no more.'

'Show me the telegram.'

The man turned. He still had his hands clenched into fists.

'I can't. There is no telegram.'

'Did you tear it up?'

'I don't remember.'

'What did it say?'

'I don't remember.'

'Why did you leave your job?'

'I don't remember.'

'Where does your former wife live?'

'I don't remember.'

'Where were you at this time a week ago?'

'I don't remember.'

'Were you here?'

'I don't remember.'

The man in the dressing gown was still standing with his back to the window and his fists clenched. His face was sweating and he looked frightened and childishly defiant. Jensen regarded him expressionlessly. After a good minute, he put his spiral-bound notepad away, took his hat and moved towards the door. Before leaving the house he said:

'Where's Department 31?'

'I don't remember.'

As he drove into the built-up area where the factory was, it was a quarter past eleven. He stopped at the police station and rang the head of the plainclothes patrol.

'Yes, they're divorced. Find out her address. Get round there and look at the diploma. If it isn't intact, bring it back with you.'

'Understood.'

'And be quick about it. I'll wait here.'

'Understood.'

'One more thing.'

'Yes?'

'He received a telegram yesterday or this morning. Put a man on to locating the copy.'

'Understood.'

The reception area was large and dreary, with yellow brick walls and plastic curtains at the windows. In the inner section there was a counter, and beyond it a series of arrest cells with shiny, barred doors. Some of them were already occupied. At the counter sat a policeman in green uniform, leafing through a report file.

Inspector Jensen sat down by the window and looked out over the square, which was empty and silent. The yellow smoke seemed to filter all the warmth out of the sun's rays and the light was flat and lifeless. The stench of the factory was awful.

'Does it always smell this bad?'

'It's even worse on weekdays,' said the

constable.

Jensen nodded.

'You get used to it. They say the fumes aren't a health risk, but my theory is, they make people depressed. Loads of them kill themselves.'

'I see.'

Fifty minutes passed, and then the phone rang.

'She was very accommodating,' said the head of the plainclothes patrol. 'Showed it to me right away.'

'And?'

'It was completely undamaged. All the sheets were there.'

'Was there anything to indicate that they might have been renewed or replaced?'

'The signatures weren't new, at any rate. The ink wasn't fresh.'

'Did you go inside the flat?'

'No, she went and fetched the diploma. Accommodating, as I say; she almost seemed to be expecting me. And a very elegant young lady, I might add.'

'And the telegram.'

'I've sent a man to the telegraph office.'

'Call him back.'

'You don't need the copy?'

'No.'

Inspector Jensen did not respond for a moment. Then he said:

'It appears to have nothing to do with the

case.'

'Inspector?'

'Yes?'

'There was one little thing that baffled me. One of my men was posted outside the building where she lives.'

'I see. Anything else?

'The police chief's been trying to get hold of you.'

'Did he leave a message?'

'No.'

The motorway was busier, and there were cars parked along the lay-bys at many points. Most of the owners were polishing the bodywork, but many had taken out the seats and were sitting on them at small folding tables beside their vehicles. On the tables they had portable TV sets and pre-packed plastic picnic baskets of the kind available from the snack vending machines. Closer to the city, the traffic queues intensified, and when Inspector Jensen reached the central district it was already ten to five.

The city was still empty of people. The football was in full swing, and those who weren't busy with their cars were indoors. The football matches were intended exclusively for broadcasting nowadays. They were played without a crowd in big, heated television studios. The teams were made up of players employed on full-time contracts, among them many foreign players, but despite the high

180

standard, interest for the matches was said to be waning. Inspector Jensen rarely watched them, but he nearly always had the television turned on when he was at home. He guessed many other people did the same.

Over the last half-hour he had been feeling increasingly light-headed, as if he was going to faint. He knew that hunger was the cause, and pulled in at a snack bar, where he purchased a cup of hot water, a small plastic sachet of instant broth mix and a portion of cheese.

While he was waiting for the soup powder to dissolve, he got out his notebook and wrote: Number 7, journalist, unmarried, age 58, left at his own request.

Even though he drank the clear soup scalding hot, it was half past five before he was back in the car, and dusk was falling as he drove west.

There were six hours left before midnight.

CHAPTER 25

It was a narrow street, and sparsely lit. It was lined with an avenue of trees and there were rows of terraced houses and bungalows down either side. He was in a district not far from the city centre. It had been built about forty years before and was inhabited mainly by civil servants, which was presumably what had saved it from being rebuilt as a standard housing estate at the time of the housing shortage.

Inspector Jensen parked the car, crossed the street and rang the bell. There was no light to be seen in the windows, and his ringing remained unanswered.

He went back to the car, sat behind the steering wheel and studied his list and notebook. Then he put them away, looked at his watch again, switched off the internal light in the car and waited.

After fifteen minutes, a short man in a velour hat and a speckled grey overcoat came along the pavement. He unlocked the front door and went in. Jensen waited until he could see light behind the blinds. Then he went over again and rang the bell.

The man opened the door at once. He was simply and correctly dressed and his appearance was in keeping with his age. His face was thin, and his eyes behind the glasses were kindly and quizzical.

Jensen showed his police ID.

'Inspector Jensen from the Sixteenth District,' he said. 'I'm conducting an investigation that has to do with your former employment and place of work.'

'Please come in,' said the man, stepping aside.

It was quite a large room. Two walls were covered in shelves of books, newspapers and

182

magazines. Under the window there was a desk with a telephone and a typewriter, and in the middle of the floor stood a low, round table and three armchairs. Light came from an anglepoise lamp at the desk and a large plastic globe above the easy chairs.

The moment Inspector Jensen came into the room, his behaviour changed. His pattern of movement was different, as were his eyes. He gave the impression of being in the middle of doing something he had done countless times before.

'Do sit down.'

Jensen sat down and got out his pen and notebook.

'What can I help you with?'

'Some information.'

'I'm at your disposal, naturally. Anything that's within my power to answer, that is.'

'When did you cease your employment?'

'At the end of October last year.'

'Had you worked for the group for a long time?'

'Relatively. Fifteen years and four months, to be precise.'

'Why did you leave?'

'Let's say I was nurturing a desire to return to private life. I left the company at my own request, by handing in my notice in the usual way.'

The man's demeanour was reserved, his voice muted and melodic.

'Can I offer you anything, Inspector? A cup of tea, perhaps?'

Jensen gave a faint shake of his head.

'What work are you engaged on now?'

'I have independent means, and therefore don't need to earn a living.'

'What do you do with your time?'

'I spend most of it reading.'

Jensen looked about him. The room was strikingly neat. Despite the large numbers of books, newspapers and other papers, everything appeared well thought out and neatly arranged, to the point of pedantry.

'When you left your employment you received some kind of diploma, or rather a farewell letter?'

'Yes, that's right.'

'Have you still got it?'

'I assume so. Do you want to see it?'

Jensen did not reply. For a full minute he sat motionless, not looking at the man. Then he said:

'Do you admit to sending an anonymous and threatening letter to the group management?'

'When am I supposed to have done that?'

'At about this time, a week ago.'

The man had pulled up his trousers and crossed his legs. He sat with his left elbow resting on the arm of the chair, and stroked his bottom lip slowly with his index finger.

'No,' he said calmly. 'I don't admit to that.'

Inspector Jensen opened his mouth to say something but appeared to change his mind. He looked at his watch instead. It said 19.11.

'I assume I'm not the first one you've spoken to in connection with this. How many people have you . . . interviewed before me?'

His tone had a bit more life in it.

'About ten,' said Inspector Jensen.

'All from the publishing house?'

'Yes.'

'What you must have had to sit through in the way of anecdotes and scabrous tall stories. Slander. Half-truths, cantankerous grumbles, insinuations. And falsified versions of events.'

Jensen said nothing.

'The whole Skyscraper is seething with that sort of stuff, from what I've heard,' said the man.

'But then perhaps that's what most places are like,' he added pensively.

'What post did you hold in your time with the group?'

'I was employed to report on culture and the arts. I held the same post, as you put it, throughout my time there.'

'Did you gain insight into the organisation and activities of the publishing house?'

'To some extent. Are you thinking of anything in particular?'

'Do you know of something called Department 31?'

'Yes.'

185

'And do you know what they do there?'

'I ought to. I spent fifteen years and four months in Department 31.'

There was a minute or so of silence, then Jensen said almost casually:

'Do you admit to sending an anonymous and threatening letter to the group management?'

The man ignored the question.

'Department 31, or the Special Department as it's also known, is the most important in the whole publishing house.'

'So I've heard people say. What does it do?'

'Nothing,' said the man. 'Absolutely nothing.'

'Explain.'

The man stood up and went to get a sheet of paper and a pencil from the meticulously tidy desk. He sat down, lined the sheet of paper up exactly with the pattern on the desktop and laid the pen parallel with the top of the sheet. Then he looked enquiringly at his visitor.

'Yes,' he said. 'I shall explain.'

Jensen looked at his watch. 19.29. The time left to him had shrunk to four and a half hours.

'Are you in a hurry, Inspector?'

'Yes. Be quick.'

'I'll try to keep it brief. You asked what the Special Department did, isn't that so?'

'Yes.'

'I've already given you a comprehensive answer: nothing. The more I develop the

186

answer, the less comprehensive it becomes. Unfortunately. Do you see?'

'No.'

'Of course not. Hopefully you will do. If not, we'll be at an impasse.'

The man said nothing for half a minute, and in that time his expression went through several changes. When he started speaking again, he seemed somehow weak and uncertain, but more committed than before.

'The simplest thing is probably for me to tell you about myself. I grew up in an intellectual home and was educated in the liberal tradition. My father was a university lecturer, and I spent ten terms at the Academy myself. The Academy had a humanities faculty back then, in more than name only. Do you understand fully what that meant?'

'No.'

'I can't explain everything. It would take us too far. It's conceivable you've forgotten the meaning of the terms I'm using, but you must have heard them at some time. Consequently, you'll gradually start to understand their implications and see the whole picture.'

Jensen put down his pen and listened.

'As I told you before, I became an arts correspondent, initially because I didn't think I had it in me to be an author. I wasn't good enough, to put it simply, even though writing was vitally important to me. It was almost my only passion.'

187

He paused. Light rain pattered on the windows.

'I worked as an arts editor on a privately owned newspaper for many years. Its pages not only provided information about art, literature, music and so on, they also left room for debate. For me, as for some other people, the debate was perhaps the most important element. It was broad in its scope, spanning virtually every aspect of society. It was often sharply critical, and not all the views expressed and points made were thoroughly thought through, not by any means.'

Jensen started to move.

'Stop,' said the man, and held up his right hand. 'I think I know what you're going to say. Yes, that's right, it did disturb people, and quite often dismayed or disappointed them, made them angry or frightened. It didn't try to placate anybody, be they institutions, ideas or individuals. We, that's to say I and a few others, thought that was only right.'

Jensen carried through his move, checking the time. 19.45.

'It's claimed,' the man said thoughtfully, 'that criticism and violent attacks would on occasion hit a person so hard that they took their own life.'

He lapsed into silence for a moment. The rain could still be heard.

'Some of us were called cultural radicals, but we were all radical of course, whether our

188

newspapers were privately owned or socialist. That didn't dawn on me until later, though. But then, politics wasn't something I took a major interest in. Besides, I mistrusted our politicians. Their qualifications often seemed inadequate to me, on both a human and an educational level.'

Inspector Jensen drummed his fingers lightly on the edge of the table.

'I know, you're waiting for me to get to the point,' the other man said mournfully. 'All right: one social phenomenon I mistrusted wholeheartedly and consistently was magazines. To my way of thinking, they had done nothing but harm for a long time. In fact, of course, they fulfilled their purpose, such as it was, and should be allowed to survive, but that certainly didn't mean they should be left to live in peace. I devoted a lot of my time to scrutinising their so-called ideology, to dissecting it and tearing it to bits. I did that in a whole series of articles, and in a polemical book.'

He allowed himself a tight little smile.

'That volume didn't make me very popular among the sort of people who cherished that kind of magazine. They called me enemy number one of the weeklies, I recall. That was a long time ago.'

The man stopped and drew a few diagrammatic sketches on the sheet of paper. The pencil strokes were fine and prim. He seemed to have a very light touch.

'Well then, let's observe the constraints of time and make a long and complicated story short and simple. The structure of society started to change, first slowly and imperceptibly, then at breakneck speed. The welfare state and the Accord were referred to increasingly often, until the two were seen as indissolubly linked and mutually dependent in every way. At first there was nothing to cause concern; the housing shortage was solved, crime figures went down; the youth question was being tackled. Meanwhile, the long-anticipated moral backlash started, as punctually as the Ice Age. Not especially worrying, as I say. Only a few of us had our suspicions. I assume you know as well as I do what happened next?'

Jensen did not answer. A strange new sensation was coming over him. It was a feeling of isolation, of seclusion, as if he and the little man with the glasses were under a plastic dome, or in a glass case in some museum.

'The most worrying thing for us, of course, was that all publishing activity was being gathered into the same camp, that publisher after publisher and paper after paper were being sold to the same group of companies, always with financial profitability as the deciding factor. It was all going well, to the point where anyone who criticised anything was made to feel like the proverbial dog barking at the moon. Even people one might have considered far-sighted began to think it carping and petty to create dissent around issues on which there was really only one view. I was never with them on that one, though that may have had something to do with my obstinate, monomaniac streak. A tiny number of cultural workers, that was the term they used then, reacted the way I did.'

There was complete silence in the room. The sound from outside had stopped.

'Even the paper I worked on was sucked in by the group, of course. I can't remember exactly when it happened. I mean, there was an apparently endless series of fusions and dummy buyouts, and not much was written or said about it. Even before that, my section had been cut right down. In the end it was scrapped altogether, dismissed as unnecessary. That meant in practice I had no way of earning a living, like a number of colleagues from other papers and various freelance writers. For some reason it was only the most stubborn and pugnacious of us who couldn't be found new positions. I didn't realise why until much later. Sorry, I must just get a drink. Do you want anything?'

Jensen shook his head. The man stood up and disappeared through a door that presumably led to the kitchen. He came back with a glass of mineral water, drank a few mouthfuls and set it down.

191

'They'd never have made a sports reporter or TV reviewer of me, anyway,' he muttered.

He lifted the glass a few centimetres, evidently to check it wasn't leaving a ring on the tabletop.

'A month or two went by, and the future didn't look very bright in practical terms. Then one day I was invited in to the big publishing house to discuss possible employment, to my utter astonishment.'

He paused again. Jensen checked the time. 20.05. He hesitated for a moment and then said:

'Do you admit to sending an anonymous and threatening letter to the management?'

'No, no, not yet,' the man said in irritation.

He took a drink of water.

'I went there full of scepticism, and was confronted with the management of the time, which was in fact more or less the same as today's. They were extremely accommodating, and the proposal they made me took me totally unawares. I can still remember how they worded it.'

The man gave a laugh.

'Not because I've a particularly good memory, but because I wrote it down. They said that free debate mustn't be allowed to die, or its practitioners be left to sink into inactivity. That even with society well on its way to perfection, there would always be issues to be discussed. That free debate, even

192

if it was superfluous, was one of the primary requirements for the ideal state. That existing culture, in whatever form, had to be nurtured and preserved for posterity. Finally they said that the group, having now assumed responsibility for such a large proportion of the country's most vital publishing activity, was also prepared to take responsibility for the cultural debate. That they planned to publish the country's first all-round, completely independent cultural magazine, with the aid of the best and most spirited people in the business.'

The man seemed to be getting more and more carried away by his subject. He tried to catch Jensen's gaze and hold it.

'They treated me very correctly. Dropped a few respectful insinuations about my frequently aired views on the weeklies, shook hands with me as if the whole thing were some kind of table tennis match, and said they were looking forward to confounding all my preconceptions. They rounded it all off with a concrete offer.'

He sat there for a while, apparently absorbed in his own thoughts.

'Censorship,' he said. 'There's no official censorship in our country, is there?'

Jensen shook his head.

'Yet I can't help feeling the censorship here is more implacable and thorough than it can ever be in a police state. Why? Because it's implemented privately, of course, in an entirely unregulated fashion, using methods that are legally unimpeachable. Because, mark my words, the practical possibility of censoring things, as distinct from the right to do it, lies with people—be they civil servants or individual businessmen—who are convinced their decisions are right, and to the benefit of all. And because most of the ordinary people also believe in this absurd doctrine and consequently censor themselves, whenever the need arises.'

He threw Jensen a quick glance, to check his audience was following.

'Everything's censored: the food we eat, the papers we read, the TV programmes we watch, the radio broadcasts we hear. Even the football matches are censored; they say they edit out any situations in which players are injured or infringe the rules in a major way. It's all done for the good of the people. You could see the way it was all going from a very early stage.'

He drew a few more geometric figures on his piece of paper.

'Those of us who were concerned with the debate on cultural issues noticed the tendency long ago, though it only showed itself at first in contexts that weren't really in our area. The symptoms were most obvious in the judicial system. It started with the secrecy laws being applied more often and more rigorously; the military managed to persuade the legal profession and the politicians that all sorts of petty little things might compromise national security. Then we started to notice that other cases were also increasingly being heard behind closed doors, a practice I've always considered dubious and objectionable, even when the accused happens to be a sex maniac. In the end, almost every trifling case was being heard wholly or partly out of reach of the individual members of the public. The motivation was always the same: to protect the individual from offensive, inflammatory or alarming facts that might have an impact on his or her peace of mind. At the same time it became clear—I still remember my amazement when I first discovered it— that a number of fairly high level state and local government officials had the authority to use the secrecy laws in connection with any enquiries pertaining to their own administrative bodies. Absurdly non-crucial matters, like where the local authority was to tip its rubbish and things like that, came under the Official Secrets Act and nobody turned a hair. And within the branches of business that were controlled by private capitalism, and newspaper publishing above all, censorship was deployed still more relentlessly. Usually not maliciously or to evil ends, but on the basis of something called moral responsibility.'

He finished his mineral water.

'As for the moral qualifications of the people who wielded that power, the less said on that subject the better.'

Jensen looked at his watch. 20.17.

'The moment the union movement and the private-sector employers reached unanimity, it created an unprecedented concentration of power. Organised opposition melted away.'

Jensen nodded.

'After all, there was nothing to oppose. All the problems were solved, even the housing shortage and the terrible parking situation. Everyone was becoming materially much better off, fewer children were being born outside marriage, fewer crimes were being committed. The only people who could possibly oppose or criticise the identikit political alliance that had achieved this economic and moral miracle were a handful of suspicious professional polemicists like myself. The sort who could be expected to ask lots of irrelevant questions. At what cost was this material luxury being won? Why were fewer children being born outside marriage? Why was criminality declining? And so on.'

'Get to the point,' said Inspector Jensen.

'Yes of course, the point,' the man said drily. 'The concrete offer they made me was extremely tempting. The group was planning to publish this formidable magazine, as I said. It was to be written and edited by the best, the most explosively and dynamically thinking

196

cultural figures in the country. I remember that exact wording. I was judged to belong in that category, and I can't deny I felt flattered. They showed me the list of names of those who would be editing it. It surprised me, because the team they'd assembled, about twenty-five of them, amounted to what I would have termed at the time the cultural and intellectual elite of the nation. We would have every conceivable resource at our disposal. Do you see why I was surprised?'

Jensen watched him with indifference.

'Naturally there were a few provisos. The magazine would have to make a profit, or at least break even. That was one of their articles of faith, after all. The other was that everyone was to be protected from evil. Well, if it was going to make a profit, the magazine would have to be planned very carefully; the definitive form and design had to be put in place. Before that, a series of market research projects would have to be conducted; we could reckon on producing a long series of fully edited sample issues. Nothing was to be left to chance. As regards the content and the subjects raised, we were to have a completely free hand, of course, both in the testing stage and later, when the magazine was launched on the open market.'

He smiled a grim smile.

'They also said that one of the basic rules in their line of business was complete secrecy for any new publication in its projection and development phase. Otherwise someone else, God knows who, might steal the whole idea. They also pointed out that it had, for example, taken years for some titles— they named various ghastly titles from their standard range—to reach their definitive form. This was to support their advice that more haste might mean less speed, and that we should go about things cautiously and with the greatest discretion, to achieve a perfect result. It was an astonishingly advantageous offer. Within reasonable limits, I was to set my own salary. The salary we agreed was to be paid in the form of a fee for each piece I wrote, which would be entered in the accounts. Even if those fees didn't amount to the total agreed in advance, that sum would be paid out anyway. Admittedly this might lead to a certain imbalance, meaning that at times I might technically be in debt to the publishing house, or vice versa. Then it would be up to me to restore the balance. If I was in deficit, I could make it up by producing more material; if I had over-produced I would have a chance to take a rest. The remainder of the contract was just routine clauses: I could be fired if I misbehaved, or deliberately sabotaged the group's interests; I was not to leave my employment without paying off any money potentially owing, and various things like that.'

The man fiddled with his pencil, but without

moving it from its position.

'I signed. The agreement gave me a far higher income than I'd ever had before. It turned out later that everyone had signed the same type of contract. A week later I started work in the Special Department.'

Jensen opened his mouth to say something, but decided against it.

'That was the official name, the Special Department. The Department 31 label came later. We were put on the thirty-first floor, you see, at the very top of the building. The rooms up there had originally been intended as some kind of storage or loft area; hardly anyone knew they were there. The lifts didn't go up that far and the only way up was via a narrow metal staircase, spiral steps. There were no windows, either, but there were a few skylights in the roof. The reason we were up there was twofold, they said. Partly so we could work completely undisturbed, partly so it would be easier to keep the project secret through the planning stage. We worked different hours to everybody else in the group, shorter hours in fact. It all seemed plausible at the time. Does that surprise you?'

Jensen did not answer.

'So we started work, with a good deal of friction initially; you can just imagine two dozen individualists, with minds of their own and without an existing common denominator. The person in charge was a complete illiterate

199

who later got one of the most senior jobs in the whole group of companies. I can add to your store of anecdotes by telling you he's said to have got top journalist posts because he's dyslexic, just like the chairman and the publisher. He kept a low profile, though. The first sample issue didn't go to print for eight months, largely because the technical production side was so slow. It was a good, bold issue, and to our complete amazement the management received it very positively. Despite the fact that lots of the articles were critical of almost everything, including the weekly press, they made no comment on the content. They just urged us to adjust a long list of technical details, and above all to step up the rate of production. Until we could guarantee a new issue every fourteen days, regular publication was out of the question. Even that sounded plausible.'

He bestowed a kindly look on Jensen.

'It took us two years, with the resources we had and ever more unwieldy processes of typesetting and going to press, to get into the rhythm of two issues a month. The magazine was always printed. We would be given ten sample copies of every issue. They were filed away for archival use; the need for discretion meant we were strictly forbidden to take copies out of the office. Well, when we'd got that far, the management seemed satisfied, delighted even, and they said all that was needed now was to give the magazine a new layout, a modern design to enable it to stand on its own in the competitive climate of the open market. And believe it or not, it wasn't until that redesign, which was in the hands of strange groups of experts, had been going on for eight months with no visible results, that—'

'That what?' said Inspector Jensen.

'That the full implication of what they were up to finally dawned on us. When we started to object, they placated us by printing bigger runs of sample issues, up to about five hundred, that were to be sent out to all the daily papers and important authorities. We gradually realised it was all a complete sham, but it took us a while. It was only as we slowly became aware that the magazine's name was never mentioned and its content was never discussed that we realised copies were never actually distributed at all. That the magazine was only used as a correlative, or rather as an indication of what and how one was allowed to write. We always got our ten copies. Since then . . .'

'Yes?'

'Since then the whole awful thing's just carried on, basically as before. Day after day, month after month, year after year, this country's cultural elite, the last of their kind, have sat in their ghostly offices dutifully but ever less enthusiastically putting together a magazine that's still, in spite of everything, the only one in this country worthy of the name.

And it's never published! Over the course of that time they've had a hundred different excuses for why it has to be that way. The latest design wasn't acceptable; the rate of production was too slow; there wasn't enough capacity in the presses. And so on. The only thing they've never had any problem with is the actual content.'

He tapped the edge of the table with the middle finger of his right hand.

'And that content could have changed everything. It could have made people aware of things before it was too late, it could even have saved a lot of them. I know that's true.'

The man suddenly raised his hand, as if to break off a reply that had never begun.

'I know, you're going to ask me why we didn't leave. The answer's simple: we couldn't.'

'Explain.'

'Gladly. The way our contracts were drawn up meant we were soon in terrible debt to the group. By the end of the first year, I owed the company more than half the money I'd earned. After five years the sum had increased fivefold, after fifteen it was astronomical, at least for people in ordinary financial circumstances. The debt was a so-called technical one. We were sent regular statements of how much it had grown by. But no one ever demanded that we pay it back. Not until the moment any of us tried to leave Department 31.'

'But you were able to leave anyway?'

'Only thanks to a complete fluke. I inherited a fortune, out of the blue. Although it was vast, almost half of it went on paying my debt to the publishing house. A debt, incidentally, that they managed to keep ramping up by various tricks until the very moment I wrote the cheque. But I was free. Even if it had cost me my entire inheritance, I'd still have torn myself free. Once I'd scented freedom I'd probably even have robbed or stolen to get the money together.'

He laughed.

'Robbing and stealing, they're a couple of disciplines without many practitioners these days, eh?'

'Do you admit that you—'

The man instantly interrupted him.

'Do you understand the full implication of what I've been saying? This is murder, intellectual murder, far more loathsome and distasteful than the physical kind. The murder of countless ideas, the murder of the capacity to form an opinion, of freedom of expression. First-degree murder of a whole cultural sector. And the motive was the lowest of them all: guaranteeing people peace of mind, to make them inclined to swallow uncritically the rubbish that's forced down them. Do you see: spreading indifference without opposition, injecting a compulsory dose of poison after first making sure there's no doctor and no antidote.'

He gabbled all this with great vehemence, and went straight on, not even pausing for breath:

'You may argue, of course, that we all did very nicely out of it, apart from the nine who went out of their minds or dropped down dead or killed themselves. And that it cost the group a lot of money to pretend to publish a magazine it never published. Bah, what's money to them, with their accountancy lawyers who also happen to work at the tax office . . .'

He stopped himself, and seemed suddenly tranquil.

'Sorry for having sunk to that kind of argument. Yes, of course I admit it. You knew I would, from the very start. But I wanted to explain a few things first, and it was also a sort of experiment on my part. I wanted to see how long I could avoid conceding it.'

The man smiled again and said casually:

'I lack talent when it comes to not telling the truth.'

'Be more specific about the motive for what you did.'

'Once I'd wrenched myself free, I wanted to draw at least some attention to what was going on. But I soon realised that my hope of writing something and getting it published somewhere or other was a vain one. In the end I decided there might conceivably still be some kind of reaction to events of a brutal and sensational nature. That was why I sent

204

the letter. I was wrong, of course. That very day I had permission to visit one of my former colleagues in the mental hospital just opposite the head office. I stood there watching the police close off the area and the fire brigade arrive and the whole Skyscraper being evacuated. But not a word was said or printed about the incident, and as for any kind of analysis, forget it.'

'Are you prepared to repeat your confession in the presence of witnesses? And to sign a statement?'

'Of course,' the man said absently. 'In any case, you'd have no difficulty finding all the technical evidence you might need. Right here in this house.'

Jensen nodded. The man got to his feet and went over to one of the bookshelves.

'I'd like to present some technical evidence, too. This is an issue of the magazine that doesn't exist. The last one we produced before I left.'

The magazine was a sober piece of workmanship. Jensen leafed through it.

'Though the years wore us down, we didn't get so toothless that they dared to let us go,' said the man. 'We tackled all sorts of issues. Nothing was taboo.'

The magazine's content was astounding. Jensen's expression remained entirely deadpan. He stopped at a double-page spread that seemed to be about the physical aspects of the falling birth rate and the decline of sexuality. Two large pictures of naked women flanked the text. They were evidently meant to represent two types. One was reminiscent of the pictures in the sealed envelope he had found in the chief editor's desk drawer: a smooth, straight, well-nourished body with narrow hips and shaven or non-existent pubic hair. The other picture was of Number 4, the woman in whose flat he had been standing twenty-four hours before, leaning on the doorpost and drinking a glass of water. She had big, dark nipples, broad hips and a rounded belly. From between her legs protruded a luxuriant patch of black hair, spreading up across the lower part of her abdomen. Even so, the genitals were visible; they seemed to be protruding from the angle between her thighs.

'That's a newly taken photo,' the man commented. 'We wouldn't settle for anything less, but it was hard to get. That type's apparently even more of a rarity now than it was before.'

Jensen flicked on through the pages. Closed the magazine and looked at the time. 21.06.

'Fetch your wash things and come with me,' he said.

The little man with the glasses nodded.

Their conversation was concluded in the car.

'There's one more thing I must confess to.'

206

'What's that?'

'They're going to get an identical letter at the same time tomorrow. I'd just been out to post it when you came.'

'Why?'

'I don't give up that easily. But this time I don't suppose they'll take any notice of it at all.'

'What do you know about explosives?'

'Less than the director of publishing knows about Hegel.'

'Which means?'

'Which means nothing at all. I didn't even do military service. I was a pacifist even then. If I had a whole army supply depot at my disposal I still wouldn't be able to make anything explode. Do you believe me?'

'Yes.'

Halfway to the Sixteenth District station, Inspector Jensen said:

'Did the idea of really blowing up the Skyscraper ever cross your mind?'

The man under arrest did not answer until they were turning into the gateway of the police building.

'Yes. If I'd been capable of making a bomb, and if I could have been certain no one would get hurt, then I might have blown up the Skyscraper. As it was, I had to make do with a symbolic bomb.'

As the car drew to a halt the man said, as if to himself:

'Well I've told somebody now, at any rate. A policeman.'

He turned to his companion and said:

'The trial won't be public, presumably?'

'Don't know,' said Inspector Jensen.

He switched off the tape recorder under the dashboard, got out, walked round the car and opened the door on the passenger side. He took his charge through to the body search area, went up to his room and rang the head of the plainclothes patrol.

'You've made a note of the address?'

'Yes.'

'Take two crime scene investigators and get out there. Collect all the technical evidence you can find. Be quick about it.'

'Understood.'

'One more thing.'

'Yes?'

'Send your chief interrogator to the solitary confinement cell. It's a confession.'

'Understood.'

Then he looked at the clock. It showed twenty-five to ten. There were two hours and twenty-five minutes left until midnight.

CHAPTER 26

'Jensen? What have you been doing?'

'Completing the investigation.'

'I've been trying to get hold of you for two days. Matters have taken a new turn.'

Jensen said nothing.

'And what do you mean by completing?'

'The guilty party has been taken into custody.'

He could hear the police chief's heavy intake of breath.

'Has the person in question confessed?'

'Yes.'

'Entirely convincing?'

'Yes.'

'Linked to the crime?'

'Yes.'

The police chief seemed to be thinking.

'Jensen, the group chairman must be informed immediately.'

'Yes.'

'You'll have to deal with it. You should probably deliver the news in person.'

'Understood.'

'Maybe it's just as well I wasn't able to get through to you any earlier.'

'I don't understand.'

'The group management contacted me yesterday. Via the minister. They thought it appropriate to break off the case. They were even prepared to withdraw their report of the crime.'

'Why?'

'We got the impression they felt the preliminary investigation had reached a dead end. Plus they were annoyed by your methods. Thought you were groping about in the dark, merely creating unpleasantness for innocent and evidently quite prominent people.'

'I see.'

'It was all very embarrassing. But since quite honestly I didn't think there was much prospect of your pulling it off within the time, I felt inclined to accept. The minister asked me straight out if I thought you had a chance. I was obliged to say no. But now . . .'

'Yes?'

'Now that's all changed, as far as I can see.'

'Yes. One other matter.'

'What's that?'

'The perpetrator has apparently written another threatening letter, just like the previous one. It ought to arrive tomorrow.'

'Is he harmless?'

'Probably.'

'Hmph, if he turns out not to be we shall be in the unique position of having caught the culprit sixteen hours before the crime is committed.'

Jensen said nothing.

'The important thing now is for you to inform the chairman of the group. You need to get hold of him now, this evening. For your own sake.'

'Understood.'

'Jensen?'

'Yes?'

'You've made a good job of it. Goodbye.'

Inspector Jensen did not leave the receiver in its cradle for more than ten seconds before he raised it to his ear again. As he dialled the number, he heard protracted, hysterical howls from down in the yard.

It took him five minutes to locate the chairman of the group at one of his country houses; five minutes later he got through. The person he was speaking to was clearly a member of the domestic staff.

'It's important.'

'The master is not to be disturbed.'

'It's urgent.'

'I can't do anything. The master has been involved in an accident and is in bed.'

'Has he got a telephone in his bedroom?'

'Yes he has.'

'Put me through.'

'I'm sorry, but I'm afraid I can't do that. The master has been involved in an accident.'

'I've got that. Let me speak to a member of the family.'

'The mistress has gone out.'

'When will she be back?'

'Don't know.'

Jensen hung up and looked at the clock, which showed a quarter past ten.

The cheese and clear soup made their presence felt in the form of heartburn, and once he had taken off his outdoor things he went to the toilets and drank a paper cup of

211

bicarbonate of soda.

The country house was located about thirty kilometres east of the city, beside the lake and in an area of relatively unspoilt countryside. Jensen drove fast, with his sirens on, and covered the distance in under twenty-five minutes.

He stopped a little way from the house and waited. As the man from the plainclothes patrol emerged from the darkness, he wound down his side window.

'Apparently there's been an accident.'

'I suppose you could call it that. He seems to be in bed, anyway. But I haven't seen any doctors. It happened several hours ago.'

'Give me the details.'

'Well, the time can't have been . . . it was dusk, at any rate.'

'Did you get some idea of what was going on?'

'Yes, I saw the whole thing. I was in a good position. Couldn't be seen myself but had a view over the terrace in front of the house, and I could see into the ground floor room, and up the flight of stairs to his bedroom. And the door up there.'

'What happened?'

'They've got guests. With young children, for the weekend apparently.' He stopped.

'Yes.'

'Small children, they may be foreign,' the policeman said pensively. 'Well, the children

212

were playing on the terrace, and he was sitting in the big room with his guests, having a drink. Alcoholic, I think, but only in moderate quantities as far as I could make out.'

'Get to the point.'

'Well, this badger comes ambling up on to the terrace.'

'And?'

'It must have lost its way. So the children start shrieking and the badger can't find its way back down, there's a kind of balustrade round the terrace and it's running up and down. The children are screaming louder and louder.'

'Yes?'

'There were no domestic staff around. And no men except for him. Oh, and me, of course. So he gets up and goes out on to the terrace and looks at the badger running up and down. The children are screaming their heads off. He hesitates at first and then he goes up to the badger and kicks it to shoo it away. The badger tosses its head and sort of snaps at his foot. And then the badger finds the way out and runs off.'

'And the chairman?'

'Well, he goes back into the house but he doesn't sit down; he goes slowly upstairs. And then I see he's opened the door to his bedroom, but he collapses just inside the doorway. Moans, and calls out for his wife. She rushes up there and guides him to the bedroom. They close the door, but I think she must be helping him get undressed. She goes out and in a few times, with various stuff like cups, a thermometer maybe, I didn't look very closely.'

'Did he get bitten by the animal?'

'Er, not bitten exactly. More like scared, I'd say. Strange.'

'What?'

'The badger, strange at this time of year, I mean. Badgers usually hibernate. I remember seeing it on that nature programme they used to have on TV.'

'Avoid superfluous comments.'

'Yes, Inspector.'

'You can return to normal duties from this point on.'

'Yes, Inspector.'

The man fingered his binoculars.

'This has been a very varied operation, if you don't mind my saying so.'

'Avoid superfluous comments. One more thing.'

'Yes, Inspector.'

'Your reporting-back technique leaves a great deal to be desired.'

'Yes, Inspector.'

Jensen went up to the house, where a maid let him in. A clock somewhere in the building struck eleven. He stood waiting, hat in hand. After five minutes, the chairman's wife appeared.

'At this time of night?' she said haughtily. 'What's more, my husband has narrowly escaped a very serious accident, and is resting in bed.'

'It's an important matter. And urgent.'

She went upstairs. She returned a few minutes later and said:

'Use the telephone over there and you can speak to him. But keep the call short.'

Jensen lifted the receiver.

The chairman sounded exhausted, but his voice was still steady and melodic.

'I see. Have you taken him into custody?'

'We've arrested him.'

'Where is he?'

'For the next three days, in the arrest cells of the Sixteenth District station.'

'Excellent. The poor fellow's mentally deranged, of course.'

Jensen said nothing.

'Has your investigation brought anything else to light?'

'Nothing of interest.'

'Excellent. Then I bid you good evening.'

'One more thing.'

'Make it quick. You've come very late and I've had a taxing day.'

'Before the man was arrested, he appears to have posted another anonymous letter.'

'I see. Do you know what's in it?'

'According to him, the wording is exactly the same as in the last one.'

Such a long silence ensued that Jensen began to think the conversation was over. When the chairman finally spoke, his vocal pitch had changed.

'So he's threatening another bomb attack?'

'Apparently.'

'Could he have had the occasion or opportunity to smuggle an explosive device into the building and hide it there?'

'It seems unlikely.'

'But it can't be entirely ruled out?'

'Naturally not. It can be viewed as extremely unlikely, however.'

The chairman's tone had grown thoughtful. After a thirty-second pause, he concluded the call by saying:

'The man's clearly deranged. It all seems most unpleasant. But if there are any steps to be taken, it can scarcely be done until tomorrow, can it? I wish you a good evening.'

Jensen drove slowly, and at midnight he was still some fifteen kilometres from the city. Very soon afterwards he was overtaken by a big black car. It looked like the chairman's, but he couldn't be sure.

It was two by the time he got home.

He was tired and hungry, and lacked that sensation of relative satisfaction he generally experienced when he wrapped up a case.

He got undressed in the dark, went out to the kitchen and poured about fifteen centilitres of spirits into a glass. Then he drank

216

the lot in one go, standing by the sink, rinsed the glass and went to bed.

Inspector Jensen fell asleep almost at once. His last conscious impression was a sense of isolation and discontent.

CHAPTER 27

Inspector Jensen was wide awake the instant he opened his eyes. Something had woken him but he didn't know what. It could hardly have been an external phenomenon like a shout or the ringing of a telephone. It was more as if his sleep had been penetrated by a thought as sharp and bright as a flashlight, though it disintegrated as he opened his eyes.

He lay there on his back in bed, looking up at the ceiling. The electric clock showed five minutes to seven and it was Monday.

Jensen got a bottle of mineral water out of the refrigerator, poured it and went over to the window with the glass in his hand. The scenery outside was scrubby, grey and depressing. He finished the mineral water, went into the bathroom and filled the bathtub, took off his pyjamas and got in. He lay there in the hot water until it started to cool; then he stood up, showered, towelled himself dry and got dressed.

He did not bother to read the morning

paper but ate three rusks with his hot water and honey. They had no effect to speak of, leaving him emptier than ever, with a wild, painful, churning hunger.

Although he kept to a moderate speed on the motorway, he almost went through a red light at the bridge and had to slam on the brakes. The cars behind hooted their reproaches in unison.

At exactly half past eight he entered his office, and two minutes later the telephone rang.

'Did you speak to the group chairman?'

'Yes, on the phone. He was indisposed. He'd gone to bed.'

'What was wrong with him? Was he ill?'

'A badger gave him a scare.'

The police chief said nothing for a bit, and Jensen was left listening to his uneven breathing as usual.

'Well it plainly can't have been that serious. Early this morning the chairman and the publisher both took a plane to some conference abroad.'

'And?'

'That wasn't why I rang. I wanted to tell you your worries are over this time round. I assume all the paperwork's in order?'

Jensen leafed through the reports on his desk.

'Yes,' he said.

'The state prosecutor's given this one

priority treatment. His people will be coming to fetch the man from the arrest cells in about ten minutes to put him into detention on remand. This is the appropriate time for you to send along all the reports and interview transcripts relevant to the case.'

'Understood.'

'As soon as the public prosecutor's office has assumed responsibility for the man you can close the case and log it. Then you and I are both free to forget the whole thing.'

'Understood.'

'That's fine then, Jensen. Goodbye.'

The men from the public prosecutor's office arrived at the appointed time. Inspector Jensen stood at the window and watched as they took their charge out to the car. The man in the velour hat and the speckled grey overcoat appeared unconcerned, and looked curiously around the concrete yard. All there was to see were hoses, buckets and a couple of constables from the sanitary squad in rubber boiler suits of a sulphurous yellow.

The two guards seemed to be taking their task very seriously. They had not put handcuffs on the man and were not holding his arms, but were keeping close on both sides, and Jensen observed that one of them kept his right hand in his overcoat pocket the whole time. Presumably he was new to the job.

Jensen stayed there at the window for a long

time after the car drove off. Then he sat down at his desk, took out his spiral-bound pad and read through his notes. At several points he paused for a long time, or turned back to something he had just read.

When the wall clock announced the time with eleven short rings he put down the pad and stared at it for thirty minutes. Then he put it in a brown envelope, which he sealed. He wrote a number on the back of the envelope and put it in the bottom drawer of his desk.

Inspector Jensen stood up and went down to the canteen. On the way he gave automatic answers to the greetings of other staff.

He ordered the set lunch, received a loaded tray and took it over to the corner table that was always reserved for him. The lunch comprised three slices of meatloaf, two baked onions, five overcooked boiled potatoes and a limp lettuce leaf, all covered in a thick, starchy sauce. Then half a litre of homogenised milk, four slices of dry bread, a portion of vitamin-enriched vegetable margarine, a piece of processed cheese, a mug of black coffee and a gooey iced cake with candied fruit on top.

He ate slowly and systematically and did not seem quite there, as if the whole procedure was nothing to do with him.

When he had eaten the lot he picked his teeth carefully, taking his time. Then he sat completely still, with a straight back and his hands resting on the edge of the table. He did not seem to be looking at anything in particular, and those passing his table could not catch his eye.

After half an hour he went up to his office and sat down at his desk. He looked through some routine files that had come through about the latest suicides and alcoholic cases, and pulled one from the file. He tried to read it but found it hard to concentrate.

He was sweating copiously and his thought processes were becoming undisciplined, breaking through barriers in a way they very rarely did.

The lunch was too much for his defective digestion.

He put down the report and got up, crossed the corridor and went into the toilet.

Inspector Jensen shut the door, stuck his middle and index fingers down his throat and threw up. The contents of his stomach felt acidic and wrong, and after a while it did not come up so readily.

He knelt in front of the toilet bowl and gripped it, and as he was being sick he thought someone could come through the door and shoot him from behind. If the person shooting had a good revolver, the back of his head would be blown away and he would be thrown headlong over the toilet and that's how they would find him.

As the convulsions abated, his thoughts

returned to their ingrained courses.

Once he had had a wash, he splashed his wrists and the back of his neck with cold water. Then he combed his hair, brushed down his jacket and returned to his office.

CHAPTER 28

Inspector Jensen had just sat down when the telephone rang. He lifted the receiver, glancing at the clock from force of habit. 13.08.

'Jensen?'

'Yes.'

'They've had the letter, just as you predicted.'

'Yes?'

'The head of publishing has just contacted me. He sounded doubtful and worried.'

'Why?'

'As I told you, the chairman and publisher are both out of the country. So he's in sole charge over there, and he doesn't seem to have been left any particular instructions.'

'About what?'

'About the steps he should take. He evidently wasn't warned to expect the letter. It hit him like a bomb, so to speak. I got the impression he wasn't even aware the culprit had been caught.'

'I see.'

'He asked me over and over again whether it really was a hundred per cent certain there was no explosive device in the building. I told him the risk seemed very small, at any event. But guaranteeing something, anything at all, one hundred per cent, could you do that?'

'No.'

'Anyway, he wants some men there to help out in any eventuality. And we can hardly refuse him that.'

'I see.'

The police chief cleared his throat.

'Jensen?'

'Yes.'

'There's no call for you to go over there personally. For one thing you've had a trying week, and for another, it's virtually a matter of routine this time round. And besides . . .'

He paused for a moment.

'The head of publishing didn't seem exactly delighted at the prospect of seeing you again. Let's not go into why that might be.'

'No.'

'Send the same manpower as before. Your right-hand man knows the details of the case now. Let him take command.'

'Understood.'

'That naturally doesn't imply any kind of repudiation of you, I hope you realise. But there's no reason not to show a certain amount of flexibility, when the occasion arises.'

223

'I see.'

Jensen sounded the alert as he was instructing the head of the plainclothes patrol.

'Be discreet. Avoid creating any kind of disturbance.'

'Yes, Inspector.'

He hung up and heard the bell ringing on the ground floor.

Ninety seconds later, the cars were moving out of the yard. It was 13.12.

He sat there for a minute more and tried to muster his thoughts. Then he got to his feet and walked the few steps to the radio control centre. The policeman at the switchboard got up and stood to attention. Inspector Jensen took his place.

'Where are you?'

'Three blocks from the Trades Union Palace.'

'Turn off your sirens once you're through the square.'

'Understood.'

Jensen's voice was calm and normal. He did not look at the clock. He knew the timings already. The head of the plainclothes patrol would reach the building at 13.26.

'Just through the square. I can see the Skyscraper now.'

'No uniformed personnel inside, or in the immediate vicinity of, the building.'

'Understood.'

'Station the flying squad officers and

vehicles three hundred metres from the building, half at each approach road.'

'Understood.'

'Increase the spacing between the vehicles.'

'Done.'

'Follow the same timetable as last week.'

'Understood.'

'Contact me as soon as you've made your assessment. I'll be waiting here.'

'Understood.'

Jensen stared at the control panel in silence.

The Skyscraper was among the tallest buildings in the country, its elevated position making it visible from all over the city. You could always see it there above you, and whatever direction you were coming from, it seemed to be the point towards which your approach road was leading. It had a square ground plan and was thirty-one floors high. Each of its façades had four hundred and fifty windows and a white clock with red hands. Its exterior was of glass, the panes dark blue at ground level, fading gradually to lighter shades on the higher floors. The Skyscraper enlarged to fill his entire field of vision.

'I'm there now. Over and out.'

'Over and out.'

Inspector Jensen looked at his watch. 13.27.

The radio operator flicked the switch.

Jensen did not move and kept his eyes on the clock face. The second hand ate up the time in quick little jerks.

225

There was total silence in the room. Jensen's face was tense and focused; his pupils had shrunk, and there was a network of fine lines round his eyes. The operator gave his superior an enquiring look.

13.34 . . . 13.35 . . . 13.36 . . . 13.37 . . .

The radio apparatus crackled; Jensen didn't move a muscle.

'Inspector?'

'Yes.'

'I've seen the letter. There's no doubt it was put together by the same person. Same types of lettering and everything. Only the paper's different.'

'Go on.'

'The man I spoke to, the head of publishing, he was terribly on edge. Clearly petrified something might happen while the bosses are away.'

'And?'

'They're evacuating the whole building, just like last time. Four thousand, one hundred people. The evacuation's already started.'

'Where are you?'

'Outside the main entrance. The people are flooding out.'

'The fire brigade?'

'Alerted. One fire engine. That'll do for backup. Excuse me . . . I must just sort out the road closure. I'll get back to you.'

He heard the head of the plainclothes patrol giving orders to someone. Then it all went

226

quiet.

13.46. Inspector Jensen was still sitting there in the same position. His expression was unchanged.

The radio operator shrugged and stifled a yawn.

13.52. The speaker crackled again.

'Inspector?'

'Yes.'

'It's thinning out. It was quicker this time. These ought to be the last ones, just coming out now.'

'What's the situation?'

'All in order. The road closure's a hundred per cent effective. We're blaming it on a fault in the district heating. The fire engine's here. It's all going fine.'

The head of the plainclothes patrol sounded calm and assured. His tone was almost relaxed, almost soothing.

'Jesus, what a lot of people. Like a horde of army worms. They're all out now.'

Jensen's eyes followed the second hand, round and round and round. 13.55.

The radio operator yawned.

'Lucky it's not raining,' said the head of the plainclothes branch.

'Avoid unnec—'

Inspector Jensen gave a sudden start and half rose from his chair.

'Have all the staff left the building? Answer concisely.'

'Yes, apart from a small Special Department. They say it's in a well-protected position and tricky to evacuate at such short notice.'

The pattern was all falling into place. He saw everything very clearly as if in the glare of a magnesium flash. Jensen sat back down while the other man was speaking.

'Where are you?'

'Just outside . . .'

'Get into the entrance hall. Be quick about it.'

The light flash died. Inspector Jensen knew what he had been thinking for that fraction of a second, the instant he woke up.

'Yes, Inspector.'

'Quick, the telephone at the security desk. Dial Department 31. You'll see the list of numbers in front of you.'

Silence. 13.56.

'The phone's . . . dead, I got the number . . .'

'The lifts?'

'The whole electrical system's shut down. Telephones and everything.'

'To run upstairs. How long?'

'Don't know. Ten minutes.'

'Have you got anyone in the building?'

'Two men, but neither of them higher than the fourth floor.'

'Call them down. Don't answer me. You're short of time.'

13.57.

'They're coming down.'

'Where's the fire engine?'

'Outside the front entrance. My men are here now.'

'Get it round the corner of the annexe.'

'Done.'

13.58.

'Take cover. Behind the annexe. Run.'

A crackle of heavy, panting breath.

'Is the building empty?'

'Yes . . . apart from those . . . thirty-first.'

'I know. Press yourself against the wall, out of range of falling debris. Open your mouth. Let yourself go slack. Think about your tongue. Over and out.'

13.59.

Jensen flicked the switch.

'Major incident alert,' he told the radio operator. 'Don't forget the helicopter branch. Be quick about it.'

Inspector Jensen got up and went back to his office.

He sat down at his desk and waited. He sat utterly still and wondered if he would hear the bang from there.

Chivers Large Print Direct

If you have enjoyed this Large Print book and would like to build up your own collection of Large Print books and have them delivered direct to your door, please contact **Chivers Large Print Direct**.

Chivers Large Print Direct offers you a full service:

☆ **Created to support your local library**

☆ **Delivery direct to your door**

☆ **Easy-to-read type and attractively bound**

☆ **The very best authors**

☆ **Special low prices**

For further details either call Customer Services on 01225 443400 or write to us at

Chivers Large Print Direct
FREEPOST (BA 1686/1)
Bath
BA1 3QZ